HEROES OF THE KALEVALA

HEROES
OF THE
KALEVALA
FINLAND'S SAGA
for young readers
BY BABETTE DEUTSCH

ILLUSTRATED BY FRITZ EICHENBERG

GREENPOINT BOOKS

Cover design
by Michael Schrauzer

TO MICHAEL

with his mother's love

NOTE

THE stories retold here were first composed in time beyond memory by people living in that part of the north which is now called Finland, and in neighboring countries. It was the custom for singers to wander about from place to place, chanting legends and folk-tales to the music of the kantele, a rude sort of harp, before the chiefs of clans and even in the huts of the poor. A little more than a hundred years ago Dr. Elias Lönnrot, a country doctor who loved these ballads, traveled the length and breadth of Finland, visiting those who remembered the old songs, collected them and set them down in writing, in the language in which they were composed. He believed, mistakenly, that they formed a single epic, like the Iliad, and he pieced them together in a poem called the Kalevala. The word may be roughly translated as Land of Heroes, and was sometimes used as a name for Finland. The North Country, or Pohjola, which is referred to so often in the poem, is believed to be Lapland. The metre employed by Lönnrot has been made familiar to us by Hiawatha, a work which draws largely upon the Finnish epic. The Kalevala has been translated into several languages, perhaps the more faithful of the English versions being that of W. F. Kirby, which was published in 1907. The original is made up of fifty runes or cantos. They tell the story of Vainamoinen, the great singer and magician, together with other more or less related tales, and such legends as the myth of the creation of the world. In order to make the story more coherent, the present writer has altered the arrangement slightly, shortened a few passages, and omitted some details. The effort throughout has been to preserve as nearly as possible in a straightforward prose narrative the character of the original runes, with their mixture of the familiar and the fantastic, their marvels of magic and their homely wisdom. The writer has earnestly sought to make this text as faithful as its nature permitted to the spirit of the Kalevala.

B. D.

CONTENTS

LIST OF ILLUSTRATIONS

List of Illustrations

HEROES OF THE KALEVALA

1

THE SINGING CONTEST

LONG and long ago there lived in the North Country, which is called Pohjola, a clever youth. His name was Joukahainen and he thought himself even cleverer than he was.

In those days, when the world was new and cold, the power of a man lay not only in the strength of his arms. He must also have knowledge of many things and a fine voice. For to know the names of things and to sing well was a way of making magic. Now one thing Joukahainen was sure of, and this was that he could sing better than any maker of songs who ever lived.

One day Joukahainen made a trip to the village. There he found the old men and the girls and the old women and the young men all talking about another singer, who lived in Kalevala, the Land of Heroes. He was the oldest magician, born of the

Mother of Waters, and he had all the wisdom of the world. Lusty old Vainamoinen, they called him, and the fame of his singing had gone forth until it reached as far as the North Country.

"He can sing, oh, how he can sing!" said the young girls.

"Better songs than you know how to make, Jouka-hainen," said the young men.

"Better songs than your father taught you, Jouka-hainen," said the old men and the old women.

This made Joukahainen very angry.

He went home to his mother and told her what he had heard.

"I must go to the Land of Heroes, mother, and challenge this Vainamoinen. There is no doubt but that I shall come off best, and then everyone in the North Country will know that there is no singer greater than your son Joukahainen."

"Oh, no," said his mother.

"No, indeed!" said his father. "Vainamoinen is a most mighty singer. He will sing against you. He will sing your mouth into a snow-drift. He will sing your hands and feet into ice."

"My mother is wise," answered Joukahainen. "And my father is very wise. But I know better. I will defy this Vainamoinen. I will sing my own songs. I will

16

sing him into stone shoes. I will sing him into wooden trousers. I will sing a rock onto his shoulders and a stone onto his heart. I will sing his hands into stone gloves and his head into a helmet of stone."

Then Joukahainen went to the stable and fetched his horse. It was a wonderful horse whose mouth breathed flame and whose hooves struck sparks when he stirred. Joukahainen harnessed his horse to a golden sledge, mounted the seat, brandished his beaded whip, and thundered away.

He drove for a day, and he drove for a second day, and he drove for a third day, and on the third day he came to the sweet fields and broad heaths of the Land of Heroes.

Now it happened that lusty Vainamoinen, the oldest magician, was also driving there and on the same road. Joukahainen saw him coming but he did not stop. He drove on and he drove fast. Suddenly their sledges jammed. The shafts were wedged together and the collars of the horses were wedged together, and the reins were all tangled, and the runners were dashed to pieces. The shafts sent forth steam like smoke and the runners dripped snow-water like sweat.

So the two stopped, and looked at each other, considering.

"Who are you?" asked old Vainamoinen. "And how

17

were you brought up, that you drive on without thinking? The horses' collars are broken and the wooden
runners are broken. My sledge is smashed to pieces."

"My name is Joukahainen," answered the young
man. "But you ought to tell me who you are too. To
what race do you belong? From what low stock do you
come?"

"Young man," said the other, "if you are Joukahainen, you should move aside, for remember, you are
the younger."

"Who is younger and who is older is no concern of
mine," said Joukahainen. "All that matters is who is
wiser. Let him who knows most keep to the road, and
let the stupid yield. If you are Vainamoinen, the oldest
magician, then let us set ourselves to singing. We shall
see who can teach the other, and who is the greater
master of song."

"What sort of knowledge have I?" asked Vainamoinen. "What sort of songs can I sing? I have lived
all my life quietly among these moors, listening to the
cuckoo calling on the border of my own fields. But
never mind that. Be so good, young man, as to tell me
all that you know. Relate the sum of your wisdom."

"I know this," answered Joukahainen. "The
smoke-hole is in the roof, and the fire is on the hearth.
The seal leads a pleasant life, feeding on salmon and

herring. The pike spawns in frosty weather and the perch in the summer season.

"If this is not enough for you, I can tell you other weighty matters. In the north they plow with reindeer, and in the south with mares, and in far-off Lapland they use elk.

"I know the tall trees on Mount Pisa and the fir trees on Horna Rock.

"I know three great waterfalls and three broad lakes and three tall mountains."

"These are stories for children," said old Vainamoinen. "This is the learning of women. It is not suited to bearded men. Tell me words of deep wisdom, tell me of everlasting things."

"Very well," answered Joukahainen. "I will tell you more. I know that the titmouse is a bird and that the viper is a snake and that the ruff is a fish. I know that iron is hard and that black mud is bitter. I know that boiling water is painful, and that scorching fire hurts. I know that water is the oldest medicine, and the foam of the cataract is a magic potion. I know that the Creator of the World is a sorcerer.

"Indeed, I will tell you more. I know that water springs from the rock and that fire falls from heaven. I know that we get iron from ore, and find copper in the hills.

19

"And I will tell you more. I know that marshy country is the oldest and that the willow is the first of trees. I know that in the ancient days men made houses of pine-roots, and pots of stone."

"Is this all that you can tell me?" asked lusty old Vainamoinen, "or is it the end of your nonsense?"

"Oh, I can tell you many little things," said Joukahainen. "Well I remember the time when I plowed the ocean and hollowed out its depths. I dug caves for the fishes, I sank deep caverns in the sea. It was I who made the lakes and heaped up the high hills and formed the rocky mountains. When the earth was created it was I who planted the pillars of the sky and reared the arch of the heavens. I sent the moon on its journey and taught the sun its path and fixed a place for the Great Bear, and it was I who sprinkled the heavens with stars."

"You are a liar," said old Vainamoinen. "You have no shame. Certainly you were not present when the depths of the ocean were hollowed out and the high hills were heaped up. No one had ever seen you when the pillars of the sky were planted; no one had even heard of you when the moon was sent on its journey and the sun was taught its path and a place was fixed for the Great Bear and the sky was sprinkled with stars."

20

The Singing Contest

"If I am ignorant," retorted Joukahainen, "I will look for knowledge at the sword's point. Let us measure swords, old Vainamoinen. Let the blade decide between us, you broad-mouthed singer!"

"I am not afraid of your blade or of your knowledge," said old Vainamoinen. "I will not draw my sword on such a weakling."

This made Joukahainen angrier than ever.

"The man who will not fight," he said, "I will sing into a swine. I have overcome heroes before this. Such a man I will sing into a snouted swine and pitch him onto the dunghill in the corner of the cow-shed."

Then Vainamoinen was filled with rage. And out of his rage he began to sing.

Vainamoinen sang and the lakes swelled up and the earth shook. The hills full of copper trembled and the rocks resounded with thunder. He sang till the mountains cracked and the stones broke on the shore.

He sang of Joukahainen and of his sledge and of his horse. He sang the runners into saplings, the horse-collar into a willow-tree and the reins to branches of alder. He sang the gilded sledge into a lake among the rushes. He sang the beaded whip into a reed beside the water. He sang Joukahainen's horse to a stone.

He went on singing. He sang the golden-hilted sword to a flash of lightning. He sang the bright cross-

21

bow into a rainbow. He sang the feathered arrows into hawks in the sky. And when Joukahainen's dog lifted its muzzle he sang him into a stone.

He went on singing. He sang Joukahainen's cap into a mist and his gloves into water-lilies, and his blue coat into a fleecy cloud and his shining belt into scattered stars.

He went on singing. And as he sang Joukahainen sank into a swamp, up to his hips into a marsh, up to his arm-pits into a quicksand.

Then Joukahainen knew that the contest was ended, that his journey was over, and that he was beaten in song by the oldest magician.

He struggled to raise one foot but he could not lift it. He tried to raise the other but it was shod with stone.

"Oh, wisest Vainamoinen!" he cried. "Reverse your magic! Sing your songs backwards! Release me from torment! Loose me from this place of terror! Oh, oldest of magicians, only set me free and I will pay whatever ransom you ask."

"What will you give me," asked Vainamoinen, "if I reverse my magic, if I sing my song backwards and set you free?"

"I could give you two splendid cross-bows, one

22

swift as the wind, the other sure to hit the mark. You have only to choose between them."

"I do not want your wretched bows," said Vainamoinen. "I have plenty of them myself. All my walls are covered with cross-bows, there are cross-bows on every peg. My cross-bows go hunting in the woods all alone without any man's help."

And he sang Joukahainen deeper into the swamp.

"I could give you two splendid boats," cried Joukahainen. "One is a light racer and the other bears the heaviest loads. You have only to choose between them."

"I do not want your boats," said old Vainamoinen. "I have plenty of them myself. All the creeks are crowded with them, boats to face the gale and boats that travel against the wind."

And he sang Joukahainen deeper into the swamp.

"I have two noble stallions," cried Joukahainen. "One of them cannot be matched for speed and the other is beautiful in harness. You have only to choose between them."

"I do not want your horses," said old Vainamoinen. "I have plenty of them myself. There is a tenant for every stall in my stables. Their backs glisten like water, their haunches wear lakes of fat."

23

And he sang Joukahainen deeper into the swamp.

"Oh, old Vainamoinen, reverse your magic words, sing your songs backwards!" pleaded Joukahainen. "I will give you a golden hat, I will give you a helmet filled with silver that my father won in battle."

"I do not want your silver," said old Vainamoinen. "I have no use for your gold. I have plenty of both myself. Every store-room is crammed with treasure. Every chest overflows with gold as old as the moonlight and silver as old as the sun."

And he sang Joukahainen yet deeper into the swamp.

"Oh, old Vainamoinen, loose me from this place of terror!" cried Joukahainen. "Free me from torment, and I will give you all the corn stacked in my barns and the yield of all my fields."

"I do not want the corn in your barns," said old Vainamoinen, "and your fields are beneath my notice. I have plenty of them myself. I have fields on every side, and all are rich with stacks. My corn is the finest that grows."

And he sang young Joukahainen deeper into the swamp.

Now Joukahainen was in great misery. He was in the swamp up to his chin. His newly grown beard was

"And he sang Joukahainen yet deeper into the swamp."

bedraggled with mud, his mouth was sunk in the moss and his teeth bit on the roots of trees.

"Oh, wisest Vainamoinen," he mumbled, "oldest of magicians, reverse your magic, sing your songs backward, grant me my life, free me from this prison. My feet are sunk in the streams, my eyes smart with sand. Sing your songs backward and break the spell!

"I will give you my sister Aino. She will dust your room for you and sweep your floor, and keep the milkpots clean. And she will wash your clothes. She will weave you golden cloth and bake you cakes of honey."

Old Vainamoinen was pleased by these words. It would be a good thing to have little Aino, Joukahainen's lovely sister, to care for him in his old age. He sat down on a stone rejoicing and rested and sang. He sang for an hour, and he sang for yet another hour, and then he sang for a third hour. And he reversed the magic words and sang the songs backward and broke the spell.

Joukahainen lifted his chin out of the mud and disentangled his newly grown beard. He led his horse down from the rock and drew his sledge out of the bushes and loosed his beaded whip from the reeds. Then he mounted his sledge and hurried home to his mother.

He was full of gloomy thoughts. He clattered along with mad speed and crashed the sledge to pieces at the door.

His mother was frightened by the noise. His father was angry.

"You are a reckless fellow!" he said. "Did you break the shafts on purpose? Why do you drive so wildly and come crashing home like this?"

Young Joukahainen could not keep back the tears. He shifted his cap without a word. His lips were dry and stiff. His nose drooped sadly.

"What is wrong?" asked his mother. "Why are there tears in your eyes? Why is your mouth so stiff? Why does your nose droop?"

"There is good reason for me to be sad, mother," said young Joukahainen. "The oldest magician has beaten me. How can I keep back the tears? I must mourn all the rest of my life. I have been beaten by Vainamoinen, and what is more, I have pledged him my little sister Aino to be his wife. I have promised him my mother's darling daughter Aino, to care for him in his old age and wait on him always."

At that his mother clapped her hands.

"What are you grieving about?" she cried. "This is no cause for tears. All my life I have wished that we were kin to that high-born hero! All my days I

28

have hoped that the great singer Vainamoinen might take my daughter Aino for his wife!"

But when Joukahainen's sister Aino heard his story, she did not clap her hands for joy. She began to cry. She wept for a whole day and she wept all of the next day as well.

"What are you crying about, my little Aino?" her mother asked her. "You are a lucky girl to have won such a noble bridegroom. Vainamoinen is the greatest of singers and he is the oldest magician."

"Yes, he is an old man," said Aino sadly, and went on crying. She did not want to marry an old man, even if he were Vainamoinen, the magician.

"Stop crying, foolish girl," said her mother. "The sun shines on other doors and windows than those of your father's house. There are strawberries growing in meadows that are not your father's meadows."

But Aino went on crying.

Still crying, she wandered away into the wood, to gather twigs from which she could make bath-whisks, one for her father, one for her mother, and one for her brother, young Joukahainen.

And what strange things happened in the wood you shall hear.

2

AINO AND THE QUEEN
OF THE LAKE

THIS was summertime, when the leaves are tender, and soon Aino had plucked twigs enough to make three bath-whisks, one for her father, one for her mother, and one for her brother, young Joukahainen. So, carrying her small burden, she turned about to go home.

Now there was one in the wood watching Aino. It was none other than old Vainamoinen. And as she pushed her way through the alder-bushes he stepped out from his hiding-place.

"Lovely little Aino," he said. "How pretty you are with those silver beads round your neck and that silver cross on your breast and those blue and scarlet ribbons braided in your hair! But do not wear them, I beg you, for anyone but me."

"Not for you, and not for anyone else," retorted

Aino, "do I wear these silver beads and this silver cross and the blue and scarlet ribbons braided in my hair! Do you think I care for rich clothes from across the water, or for fine wheaten bread? I will go in plain home-spun, I will eat dry crusts, if only I can stay at home in my father's house for always and always!" And she tore the silver cross from her breast and the scarlet ribbons from her hair and threw them on the ground, and she scattered the silver beads among the bushes and ran home, crying.

Her father was sitting at the window carving the handle of a hatchet.

"So young and so sad!" he exclaimed, when he saw her. "Whatever are you crying for?"

"I have reason to cry," said Aino. "I have lost my little silver cross and my silver beads and my copper girdle."

Her brother Joukahainen was sitting at the gate, shaping sledge-runners.

"So young and so sad!" he said, when he saw her. "Whatever are you crying for?"

"I have reason to cry," answered Aino. "I have lost my little silver cross and my silver beads and my gold rings."

Her sister was sitting at the window, weaving a golden girdle.

31

"So young and so sad!" she cried, when she saw Aino. "Whatever are you crying for?"

"I have reason to cry," said Aino. "I have lost my gold and silver trinkets, and my blue and scarlet ribbons."

Her mother was at the threshold of the storehouse, skimming the milk.

"So young and so sad!" she said. "Whatever are you crying for?"

"I have reason to cry," answered Aino, and the tears fell faster than ever. "I went into the wood to gather twigs to make bath-whisks, and as I was on my way home old Vainamoinen crossed my path. He told me that I must not wear for anyone but him my silver beads and my little silver cross and my silken ribbons. I could not bear to hear him speak so, that old, old man. So I tore the cross from my breast and the beads from my neck and the blue and scarlet ribbons from my hair and threw them on the ground. I told him I did not wear them to please him or anyone else. I told him I would wear plain home-spun and eat dry crusts if only I could stay in my father's house for always and always!"

"Do not cry," said Aino's mother. "You are too young to be sad. I will tell you what to do. For a whole year you must eat fresh butter and you will grow plump. For a whole year after that you must eat rich pork and you will grow prettier. For a third year you must eat cream-cakes and you will be a great beauty. But that is not all.

"When you are full-grown and beautiful, go to the storehouse on the mountain and open the inner room. There you will find chests heaped upon chests and coffers piled upon coffers. Open the painted lid of the best coffer and there you will find six golden girdles and seven blue gowns of the finest weave, spun by the daughter of the moon and woven by the daughter of the sun. They were given me when I was young and poor, and I wore them for a day and another day and a third day, and then I laid them away in the painted chest in the storehouse on the mountain and I have not seen them from that day to this. They are waiting there for you. But that is not all.

"You must put on a shift of the finest flax and a gown of the purest wool and bind it with a girdle of silk. You must wear silk stockings and handsome slippers, and braid your hair with silken ribbons. But that is not all.

"You must slip gold rings on your fingers and golden bracelets on your wrists and put a necklace of beads round your neck and a little golden cross on your breast. And then you may come home from your visit

33

to the storehouse, the most beautiful girl in the North Country, as lovely as a mountain raspberry."

But Aino hardly heard what her mother was saying. She could not think of rich foods and fine clothes or the pleasures of being a grown girl. She could only think of how she must marry old Vainamoinen, and her thoughts were as black as pitch, her heart was no brighter than soot. She wished she had never been born or that she had died when she was a baby. She cried for a whole day, and for a second day and for a third day.

"Whatever are you crying for?" asked her mother.

"How can I help crying?" said poor little Aino. "You have promised me to an old man for his wife, to comfort him in his old age, to support his feeble steps and wait on him always. It would have been better if you had sunk me in the sea, to be a sister of the herring and a companion of the fishes. Then I would not have had to support the feeble steps of an old man, and mend his stockings."

And still crying, she went to the storehouse on the mountain and entered the inner room. She opened the painted lid of the best coffer and found the six golden girdles and the seven blue robes of finest weave. She dressed herself in silver and gold, and braided her hair with blue and scarlet ribbons.

But when she left the storehouse her heart was so heavy that she could not bring herself to go home. She wandered in the woods and among the marshes for a day and another day and a third day until she came to the borders of a wide lake. It was night when she reached it, and all that night she sat on the rocks above the lake, too sorrowful to journey further.

When dawn came she looked out over the water and saw three girls bathing there. Aino decided to join them. She took off her stockings, dropped her shoes on the stones, hung her dress on an aspen-tree and her shift on a willow branch, and threw her beads on the sand and her rings on the shingle. There was a rock in the middle of the lake that shone bright as gold in the morning light. Aino thought she would swim out to it and forget her troubles.

So she dived into the water and swam out to the rock. When she reached it she climbed up to rest a while. But she had no sooner settled on it than the rock began to sink. It sank lower and lower, and Aino with it, until it was far beneath the water.

"Alas!" cried Aino, sinking, "I went to bathe in the lake, I went to swim among the waves, and now I must die. My father dare not cast his net in this lake as long as he lives. My mother dare not draw water for cooking from this lake as long as she lives.

35

My brother dare not bring his horse to drink from this lake as long as he lives. My sister dare not wash her face in the waters of this lake as long as she lives. The water of this lake is like the blood of my veins. The fish that swim here are like the flesh of my body. The bushes beside this lake are like the ribs of me, and the grass that grows here is like my soiled and tangled hair."

So Aino sank beneath the waters. And no one knew what had become of her.

Who was to carry the sad news to her father and mother? The bear might have carried it, but he could not: he was straying among the cattle. The wolf might have carried the sad news, but he could not: he was wandering among the sheep. The fox might have carried the sad news, but he could not: he was hunting the geese. Finally the hare said, "I will take the message. I will not forget it."

So the hare hurried along on his crooked legs till he came to the home of Aino. He went directly to the bath-house, where the girls were busy with the bath-whisks.

"Come here, you scamp!" called the girls. "We'll boil you for the master's supper. Come here, Broad-Eye, we'll roast you for the breakfast of the mistress, or for her daughter's luncheon or for her son's dinner."

The hare answered boldly, "I should like to jump into the kettle and be cooked, but I have a message to deliver. Aino has sunk to the bottom of the lake. Lovely little Aino is drowned in the muddy waters. She is down there in the depths under the waves: she has become a sister of the herring and a companion of the fishes."

Now it was the turn of Aino's mother to weep and lament. The tears flowed over her cheeks and over her breast to the hem of her dress. The tears flowed over her scarlet stockings. Even her gold-embroidered shoes were wet with tears.

"Oh, unhappy mothers!" she cried. "Never urge your daughters to a marriage they do not wish! Never, never, like me, try to force your children to marry those they do not love!"

And as she cried, the tears flowed over her gold-embroidered shoes and covered the ground where she stood till it grew wet. And the tears swelled into streams, and the streams became three mighty rivers, and from the rivers rushed three raging waterfalls, and in the midst of the waterfalls rose three great rocks, and on the rocky peaks grew three lovely birch-

37

trees, and on each of the three birch-trees perched a
golden cuckoo. And the three golden cuckoos all began
singing at the same time. For three months the first
one sang: "Darling, darling!" to the poor girl under
the water. For six months the second cuckoo sang:
"Lover, lover!" to the unhappy old man who had lost
his bride. And for a whole long lifetime the third
cuckoo sang: "Joy, joy!" to the miserable mother who
would never more be joyful.

"What is the good of all my magic," said old
Vainamoinen when he heard the news, "if I cannot
win back the lovely little Aino?"

So he went to the god of dreams and asked to be
directed to the Queen of the Lake. And particularly
he asked how to reach the misty island near her oozy
kingdom under the waves. There she reigned among
her maidens, the youngest of whom was now lovely
little Aino. And the god of dreams told him.

Then old Vainamoinen took his small red boat,
and examined his fishing-tackle and looked to his
hooks, and put the tackle in his pocket and the barbed
hooks in his wallet, and made for the misty island.

As soon as he got there he began fishing. His copper
rod trembled in his hands, his silver thread whistled,
his golden line whirred. He fished for a long time.

At last, early one morning, there was a jerk at the
38

hook, and he pulled in a beautiful fish. Vainamoinen looked at it closely and turned it over and looked at it again.

"I never saw a fish like this!" he said. "It is smoother than a herring and yellower than a trout and greyer than a pike. It has not the fins of a female fish nor yet the scales of a male. It wants the hair of a girl, and yet it does not have the girdle of a water-nymph, and it is certainly not a pigeon. It is either a salmon or a deep-water perch."

So saying, old Vainamoinen took his silver-handled knife from his belt and prepared to slit the fish and cut it to pieces for his breakfast, or to make a snack for his luncheon, or to eat for dinner and get a good supper from it too.

But just as he was about to slit the fish, it leaped sideways and slipped from the planks of his red boat into the water.

It raised its head from the fifth wave and its shoulders from the sixth wave and its hands out of the seventh wave and its left foot as well, and from the ninth wave it began to speak.

"Oh, old Vainamoinen," said the beautiful creature, "I have not come here to be slit like a fish and cut to pieces like a salmon! I have not swum here to give you a breakfast or a snack for your luncheon, or to

39

provide you with a dinner and a good supper too."

"Then what did you come for?" asked old Vainamoinen.

"I came to nestle like a dove in your arm, and sit by your side always, and rest on your knee like a wife, and to prepare your bed and smooth your pillow, and to keep your room neatly and sweep your floor, and to light the fire for you and fan the flames, and to bake you three large loaves of bread and cakes of honey, and to fill your jug of beer and set your dinner for you.

"I am not a salmon, neither am I a deep-water perch. I am a young and lovely girl, Joukahainen's sister Aino, whom you wanted so much to marry. Oh, poor old Vainamoinen, how foolish you are! You had not the wit to hold me!"

"Come back, come back!" cried old Vainamoinen.

But Aino dived under the waves and he saw her no more.

Then Vainamoinen thought what he must do. He took some silk and quickly wove a net, and drew it straight and drew it across, through the quiet waters that the salmon love. He fished in the deep waters of the Land of Heroes and he fished in the dark cavernous lakes of the North Country, and he fished in the great rivers of Lapland. He caught plenty of

40

fish. But he never caught the fish he was looking for. He never caught lovely little Aino.

At last old Vainamoinen pushed his cap back on his head and said to himself, "Indeed I am a fool, and an old fool. My wisdom is failing with my strength. Lovely little Aino came to my boat and I had not the wit to hold her."

And having spoken thus, he went sadly home.

"If only," said the oldest magician, "my old mother were still alive! She would tell me how to bear my troubles, for truly I am very sad."

At those words his mother stirred in her sleep under the sea, and woke, and said:

"Your mother hears you, Vainamoinen. She has wakened to advise you. Your old mother will tell you how to bear your troubles, and put an end to your sorrow. Listen and hear. This is what you must do now.

"In the North Country there are beautiful girls, lovelier than any you might look for, and not lazy either, like the fat girls of Lapland. Get yourself a wife from among the bright-cheeked girls of the North Country, whose skin is fair and whose feet are quick. That is the advice of your old mother. That is what she woke to tell you."

So lusty old Vainamoinen resolved to travel to the

North Country, even as his mother had said, and find him a fair-haired, swift-footed girl to be his bride. He took his pea-stalk-colored mount, the blue elk, adjusted the golden bit and put on the silver bridle. Then he got on its back and started for the dark cold regions of the far north to find him a wife.

He trotted at an easy pace through the Land of Heroes, and left his home behind, and he traveled more swiftly over the sea, without even wetting his horse's hooves, and at last he came within sight of the North Country.

But in the North Country, as you remember, there lived young Joukahainen. And he was full of envy of old Vainamoinen, who had beaten him at singing, and full of anger at old Vainamoinen, because of whom little Aino had slipped away from her home to live with the Queen of the Lake. He was determined to meet old Vainamoinen again and if he met him, to kill him.

To this end Joukahainen had made himself a wonderful weapon. He had fashioned a bow of iron and overlaid the back with copper, and inlaid it with gold and silver, and carved on the back a standing horse and on the stock a running foal and on the curve a sleeping woman and on the catch a couching hare. He had made the bowstring from strong hempen

42

cord and the sinews of the elk. He had made arrows
with oakwood shafts and pinewood heads and feathered them with the plumage of swallows' wings. He
had sharpened the points well and dipped them in
poison from the black blood of adders.

His bow was fit for bending. His arrows were
ready. With his weapon in his hand and anger in his
heart he watched and waited for old Vainamoinen.
He watched at morning and at evening and again at
noon. He never grew weary waiting. He watched
from the window. He waited on the stairs. Sometimes
he lurked on the path. Sometimes he stood in the
meadow, his well-filled quiver at his back, his cross-
bow under his arm. He went further and hid near a
building. Sometimes he would go to a cape jutting
out over the water, or stand near a foaming waterfall, waiting and watching.

One day, early in the morning, as he turned his
eyes eastward he noticed a blue shape on the sea.

"Is it a cloud that I see there in the east?" Joukahainen asked himself. "Or is it a sign of day?"

But it was not a cloud and it was not a sign of day.
It was old Vainamoinen hurrying toward the North
Country on his blue elk to find him a wife.

And what happened when Vainamoinen came in
sight of his young enemy you shall hear.

43

3

WHAT BEFEL THE OLDEST
MAGICIAN

NOW when young Joukahainen saw that coming toward him was no other than the mighty singer Vainamoinen, mounted on his blue elk, he hurried to span his cross-bow. He bent it and aimed it at the head of old Vainamoinen. But before he could shoot, he found his mother standing beside him.

"Why are you spanning your cross-bow?" she asked. "What are you aiming at?"

"I am aiming at the head of old Vainamoinen," answered the young man. "I am going to shoot the famous singer through the shoulders and through the liver and through the heart. I am going to kill the oldest magician."

But his mother said, "Don't do that! You must not shoot Vainamoinen. You must not kill the hero

of the Land of Heroes. He comes of a noble race. If you shoot the famous singer, the world will be empty of joy, the earth will be bare of song."

Young Joukahainen paused a moment, though his fingers were itching to loose the shaft. He paused and considered, and then he spoke:

"What if the world were twice emptied of joy? What if the earth were bare of song forever? I will shoot anyway!"

His mother could not move him. Resolutely he spanned his iron bow, bent it against his left knee, steadied it with his foot, and drew an arrow from his quiver. It was a triple-feathered arrow, the strongest and best of them all. He laid it on the groove, fixed the hempen cord, placed his bow at his shoulder and prepared to shoot Vainamoinen.

"Now strike, my birchwood arrow!" he cried. "Twang clearly, my hempen bow-string! If my hand leans downward, then strike higher, my arrow. If my hand leans upward, then, my arrow, strike lower."

And he shot the first shaft. The arrow flew too high and went whizzing among the clouds. Reckless Joukahainen chose a second shaft. But the arrow flew too low, and sank into the earth. Then Joukahainen chose a third shaft. The third arrow flew straight and

47

buried itself in the spleen of the blue elk that was carrying old Vainamoinen.

The blue elk sank into the water and old Vainamoinen tumbled off its back and plunged into the sea. Suddenly a mighty wind arose and raised a great wave, and the wave carried old Vainamoinen out into the open ocean.

Joukahainen was filled with joy. This suited him very well.

"Now, old Vainamoinen," he cried, "as long as you live you will never again walk in the sweet fields and over the broad heaths of the Land of Heroes! You will never reach your own country. May you swim out there for six years. May you drift on the waters for seven long summers. For eight winters may you be tossed by the waves. May you float for six years like a fallen pine-tree, and for seven years like a rotten fir-tree, and for eight years like an old stump!"

Then, proud and happy, Joukahainen turned and went home. As soon as he got there his mother asked him:

"Have you shot Vainamoinen? Have you killed the son of the Land of Heroes?"

"I have shot Vainamoinen!" said the young man. "I have overthrown that old fellow from the Land of Heroes. I have sent him to swim in the sea. He is

48

tumbling about from side to side among the waves. He is drifting on his back in the water."

"You have done wrong," said his mother, "to shoot Vainamoinen. You have done very wrong."

But Joukahainen was too well pleased with himself to pay heed to anything his mother might say.

Meanwhile lusty old Vainamoinen was swimming in the open sea. He drifted like a fallen pine-tree for six summer days, and like a rotten branch of fir for six summer nights. The wide sea was spread under him. The sky was clear above him. So he swam for two more nights and for two more long dreary days. When the eighth day passed over him and the ninth night darkened about him, old Vainamoinen was in great misery. His nails were dropping from his toes. His joints were breaking in his fingers.

"Unhappy man that I am!" moaned old Vaina-moinen. "I have wandered far from my own country. I shall never reach home again. I shall drift forever under the open sky, in sunlight and in moonlight. It is a cold life I lead here out in the ocean. Indeed, I do not know how to manage. Shall I build me a house on the waters or rear me a home in the wind? If I build a house on the waters, it will drift from me on the waves. If I rear a home in the wind, the wind will blow it away."

49

As Vainamoinen mourned thus, an eagle came flying out of the northeast. He came from Lapland. He was not the largest eagle, nor yet the smallest eagle. One of his wings swept the water, and the other wing swung skyward. He rested his tail on the sea and whetted his beak on the cliffs. As he flew slowly back and forth he soon spied old Vainamoinen drifting on the blue waters.

Now the eagle knew the oldest magician from long and long ago.

Back in the beginning of the beginning, when the world was a bare island, a tiny son of earth had sown the seedlings of the first trees. One tree only had been slow to grow, and that was the oak. But then a sea-hero had arisen who had made the oak grow, and it grew and grew until it hid the sun and moon. Then another sea-hero had arisen and cut down the oak, and freed the sun and moon. The fields shone, the fruits flourished, the berries were rich and sweet, the plants were green, and the land was thick with trees. Only one thing would not grow, and that was the barley. But Vainamoinen, the oldest magician, knew what must be done. The forest must be cleared, and the land burned over, and the earth tilled, that the barley might grow. So lusty old Vainamoinen had sharpened

50

his axe and cut down all the trees of the forest and cleared the land. Only one tree he had left standing. He had spared the birch-tree so that the birds of the air might find a place to rest. This was the perch of the cuckoo. And it was the resting-place of the eagle too.

When the eagle saw Vainamoinen floating on the waters he was astonished.

"What are you doing here, oh, oldest magician," he asked, "drifting in the open sea?"

"I will tell you," said old Vainamoinen. "I went to find me a wife in the North Country. I traveled for many days, crossing the ocean on my blue elk. But when I came near to the North Country, my blue elk was shot from under me and I fell into the water. And a great gale came from the northwest and drove me out to sea. I have been swimming among the cold waves for days and days. I do not know what is to become of me, whether I shall die of hunger or whether I shall drown."

"Forget your troubles," said the eagle. "You will not drown, neither will you die of hunger. Climb up on my back and I will carry you. Well I remember the happy day, back in the beginning of the beginning, when you cleared the forest in the Land of Heroes.

51

And I remember how you left the birch-tree standing, so that the birds might rest there, and I myself might sit on its branches."

Joyfully old Vainamoinen climbed up on the eagle's back. The great bird carried him in the pathway of the wind as far as the utmost boundary of the North Country. There on the misty coast he set the old singer down, and soared into the air and left him.

But when Vainamoinen looked about him, he was distressed. He stood there all alone on the sea-coast, in a strange land. He had been beaten upon by a thousand waves. He was suffering from a thousand wounds. His beard was all disordered and his hair all tangled. He did not know which path to take or how to get home. Overcome with grief, the oldest magician lifted up his voice and wept.

Now the little servant of old Louhi, the Mistress of the North Country, had made an agreement with the sun and moon that they would always wake together and always rise together. But indeed she woke earlier than they, and before the sun and moon were up she was at her household tasks. She was busy before cock-crow, even before the cock's child began singing. Before dawn she sheared the fleece of five sheep, clipped the wool of six lambs, carded it and wove it.

What Befel the Oldest Magician

Before the sun was awake she washed the tables, swept the wide floor with her broom of leafless twigs, and collected the sweepings in her copper dust-pan. Then she took the rubbish out of doors to the field beyond the farm-yard, where there was a gap in the fence.

As she was standing there she heard a strange sound. She turned her head and listened. It was a noise of weeping that came from across the river.

She hurried home and ran into the house.

"There is someone in trouble across the river," she said to her mistress. "I heard the sound of weeping."

At that the Mistress of the North Country, old Louhi, hurried out into the farm-yard and went to the gap in the fence, and bent her ear to listen.

"This is not the cry of a child," she said. "Neither is it like the wail of a woman. This is the sound of a bearded hero weeping."

At once she got into the boat and pushed out into the water. She rowed and she rowed until she came to the spot where old Vainamoinen stood bemoaning his fate.

"Unhappy old man," said Louhi, "you are in a strange country."

"True enough," said Vainamoinen. "I am in a

53

strange country that I never saw before. I was better off in my own home. I was a greater man in my own land."

"May I ask," said Louhi politely, "from what race you are sprung? What is your noble lineage?"

"My name was well known in the old days," answered Vainamoinen. "I was famous in the old days. The sweet fields and broad heaths of the Land of Heroes knew me for my cheerful songs. I sang them every evening. I filled the valleys with them every morning. But now my heart is so heavy that I do not know myself any more."

"Come out of the marshlands," said Louhi. "And tell me your misfortunes and all your adventures."

Then she made him get into the boat and seat himself in the stern. She herself took the oars and rowed him across the river to her own house. There she fed him and warmed him. She dried his dripping clothes and rubbed his cold body with her strong hands till the blood ran freely in his veins again. When he was warm and dry and comfortable, she asked him why he had wept. So old Vainamoinen told her how he had been tossed about on the open sea, far from his home, and come at last to a strange country, where the doors were strange and the hedge-gates strange, and the pine-needles seemed to pierce him and the birch-boughs to

54

flog him, where only the wind and the sun were friendly and familiar.

"Have done with your grief, Vainamoinen," said gap-toothed Louhi, the Mistress of the North Country. "It is a good place you have come to. Here you can pass your days in comfort. There is salmon on the table and rich pork standing beside it."

"I do not relish strange food," said old Vainamoinen, "in the best of strange houses. A man is better off at home. He is a greater man in his own country. I would rather sip water from a birchbark shoe at home than drink mead out of a golden goblet in a strange land."

"Very well, then," said crafty old Louhi. "What will you give me if I send you back to your own land, to the borders of your own cornfields and the bath-house of your own home?"

"Tell me what you would like," replied old Vainamoinen eagerly. "Would you like a hat filled with silver or a helmet full of gold?"

"No," said Louhi, "I do not ask for gifts of gold or silver. Gold is a toy for children and the horses wear bells of silver. But," she said, "if you can forge the magic mill called the Sampo, I will send you safely back to your own country and besides I will give you my daughter for your wife."

"So it is a Sampo you want," said Vainamoinen.

"Yes, a magic Sampo, that can grind meal and salt and money too. I want nothing but a Sampo with its lid of many colors that turns as it grinds. I have all the materials that go to the making: the tips of a white swan's wings, the milk of a barren heifer, a single grain of barley and the fleece of a ewe's wool."

"I am sorry," said Vainamoinen. "I cannot forge a Sampo for you or weld its lid of many colors. But if you take me to my own country I will speak to my brother about it. My brother Ilmarinen is a marvellous smith. None is so handy as he. It was he who forged the heavens and laid the foundations of the air, yet you cannot see a trace of the hammer or a sign of the tongs."

"To the man who forges a Sampo with its lid of many colors I will give my daughter to be his wife," repeated Louhi.

Without further words she harnessed the colt and led old Vainamoinen to the sledge.

"Be careful," she warned him. "Do not lift your head to look about you. For if you do, evil will certainly befall you."

Vainamoinen thanked her for her kindness and mounted the sledge and flicked the white-maned horse with his whip. Noisily the sledge drove forward out of the dark misty regions of the North Country towards the home of the oldest magician.

Now Louhi's eldest daughter, the Maid of the North Country, was famed on land and sea for her great beauty. She sat on the rainbow, dressed in a garment that dazzled the eyes, and wove a cloth of gold and silver. Her shuttle was of gold and she combed her wool with a silver comb. The shuttle flew swiftly, the reel turned in her white hands, the copper shafts clattered, and the silver comb whistled as she wove her splendid cloth.

Lusty old Vainamoinen had traveled only a short distance through the dark mists of the North Country when he heard the shuttle whizzing high above him. He forgot all about Louhi's warning, and lifted his head and looked about.

And what happened after he acted in this rash fashion you shall hear.

4

THE WICKED WORK OF IRON

WHEN lusty old Vainamoinen saw the beautiful Maid of the North Country sitting on the rainbow he promptly reined in his horse.

"Climb down," he begged the dazzling girl, "and sit in the sledge beside me!"

"Why should I do that?" she demanded.

"I will tell you why," answered old Vainamoinen simply. "So that you may bake loaves of honey-cake for me and brew me the best beer, and talk to me gaily as you sit at the window, when I get back to my own country and take you into my own house."

The dazzling girl shook her head.

"Yesterday," she said, "as I was walking through the fields at sunset I heard a little bird singing. He was talking to me about getting married. And I asked him where a young woman was happier, in her father's house or in the house of a husband. And the little

"But the dazzling girl was not so easily persuaded."

bird said that a girl at home is like a strawberry in the garden, but in her husband's house a bride is like a dog that is chained."

"The bird didn't know what he was talking about," said old Vainamoinen. "At home a girl is treated like a child, but everyone has to get married some day. Climb down into my sledge. I will not make a bad husband, I am no lazier than other heroes."

But the dazzling girl was not so easily persuaded.

"I will think well of you if you do me a small favor. Only split a horsehair with a blunt knife, and tie an egg into knots for me."

The oldest magician smiled. He took a knife that had no point and split a horsehair with it, and then he quickly tied an egg into knots. And once more he begged the beautiful girl to come and sit in the sledge beside him.

"Perhaps I will," she said, "if you peel the stone I have here, and chop up a pile of ice without scattering any splinters."

These tasks were nothing to lusty old Vainamoinen. In a moment he had peeled the stone as you pare the rind from a piece of fruit, and chopped up a pile of ice without loosening a single crumb. And again he asked her to come with him.

"Not yet," said the dazzling girl. "I will not go

61

with you unless you carve me a boat from the splinters of my spindle and the fragments of my shuttle, and launch the boat on the water without touching it with your hand or pushing it with your shoulder or pressing it with your knee."

"There is no man in any country in the world who can build a boat as well as I," said old Vainamoinen proudly.

Then he took the splinters of her spindle and the fragments of her shuttle and set to work. In no time at all he had begun to shape a splendid boat. It had a hundred planks, and it stood on a hill of steel among iron rocks. He labored over it without resting for a day and another day and a third day. His axe never touched the iron rocks or rang against the steel hill.

But on the third day the Evil One, Hiisi, turned the edge of the axe-blade against old Vainamoinen. The shaft shone against the rocks, the blade rang against the steel hill. It glanced aside and struck Vainamoinen's knee and cut his toes, dealing him such a wound that the blood gushed like a torrent.

"Wicked axe!" cried the oldest magician. "You should have split a tree-trunk with your bright edge and here you have cloven my knee!"

And he began to repeat magic spells of healing. But try as he would, he could not remember the words that told how iron came to be. Now, as everyone knows, you cannot heal a wound unless you speak the words that tell the origin of the thing that inflicted the wound. Without those words, all Vainamoinen's magic was of no use. From his knee and from his foot the blood poured like a foaming river, till the berry bushes were red with blood and the heath was flooded with it.

Then old Vainamoinen limped over to the rocks and gathered lichen, and collected moss from the swamp and earth from the hillocks, hoping that with this he could staunch the flow. But for all his poulticing, the blood still ran from the great gash that the iron had made in his knee.

Vainamoinen groaned with the pain of his wound. Too late he recalled old Louhi's warning that he should not turn his head to look about him. All his spells were of no avail. He did not know what to do.

At last he mounted his sledge again, lashed his horse with his beaded whip, and drove off to find help. The sledge rocked with the speed of his going, and in a short time he came to a village where three roads met. He took the low road, drove swiftly to the house that stood lowest in the valley, and stopped at the threshold.

"Is there someone here," he shouted, "who can

cure wounds made by iron? Is there someone who can heal the hurt of a hero?"

A child was playing on the floor and a boy was sitting by the stove.

"There is no one in this house," said the boy, "who can cure wounds made by iron. There may be such people in other houses. You had better drive on."

So, with the blood still flowing from his knee, old Vainamoinen drove further. The sledge rattled along till it came to the middle road. Vainamoinen traveled until he came to the middle house, and stopped at the threshold. He looked in and shouted through the window:

"Is there someone here who can cure the wounds made by iron? Is there someone who can stop the flow of blood?"

An old woman was lying in bed, and another old woman was sitting by the stove. She gnashed her three teeth and mumbled:

"There is no one in this house who can do that. No one here knows blood-spells. You had better drive on."

So old Vainamoinen drove on. This time he took the highroad, and when he came to the house that stood at the top of the hill, he stopped at the door-post.

"Is there someone here," he called, "who can cure

wounds made by iron? Is there someone who can stop this dark red torrent?"

An old man with a grey beard was resting by the stove.

"Greater torrents than this have been stopped," he replied. "Greater floods than this have been halted by three strong words. When those words are spoken, waterfalls stop flowing, rivers stop running, and land is joined to land."

At this cheerful news, Vainamoinen jumped from his sledge, and hurried as fast as his wound allowed into the house. The servants brought a silver beaker and a golden goblet, but these could not hold all the blood that was pouring from his knee.

"Who are you?" mumbled the greybeard by the stove, watching. "Which of the heroes may you be? Here are seven large vessels brimming with blood, and eight big tubs overflowing with it, and still it gushes from your knee over the floor."

Vainamoinen told him who he was and how he had come by his terrible wound.

"I can remember other words," said the greybeard, "but I cannot recall those about the creation of iron."

Even as the greybeard spoke, Vainamoinen was reminded of how iron had come to be.

65

"If you tell me that," said the greybeard, "I will be able to tell you the spell of healing."

So Vainamoinen told him. In the beginning of the beginning three daughters of the Creator wandered across the sky, their breasts full of milk, that dropped to earth as they moved. And where the milk fell, in the swamps and the marshes and the bare mountains, it turned to ore. There Iron slept, buried in the ground, hiding from Fire, its eldest brother, fearful of Fire's bright sharp jaws. But the wolves and the bears running over the marshes tore the ground open with their claws, so that Iron could no longer remain in hiding. And then, on a hill of charcoal one dark night, the smith Ilmarinen was born, with a hammer in one hand and a pair of pincers in the other. The very day after he was born he built his smithy, and found Iron lying in the ground, and took it to his forge, and plunged it into his fiery furnace. Iron suffered torments by reason of the fire, and begged to be taken out of the furnace. But the smith was afraid that when Iron came forth he would be in a bad temper and do someone an injury. Then Iron swore by the forge and the anvil, by the hammer and the mallet, never to hurt his brother or any of his kinsmen and disgrace his relations. So the smith drew him out of the furnace. But instead of tempering Iron

66

with honey, as he meant to do, the smith was misled by the Evil One, Hiisi, and plunged Iron into a bath made of the venom of snakes and the acid of ants and the poison of toads. Then Iron, enraged, broke his oath, and instead of biting only logs of wood and breaking stone, he bit his kinsfolk and did hurt to his relations.

When the greybeard of the stove heard this story he shook his head so that his beard trembled, and said to Vainamoinen:

"Now I know how Iron was created. Now I know his evil habits. Oh, wicked Iron," said the greybeard, "when you dropped to earth as milk and turned into ore you were neither great nor little. But when Ilmarinen drew you out of the furnace and tested you and tempered you, then you grew proud and evil, and broke your solemn oath, and brutally bit your brother and struck at your own relations, and made the blood gush out in torrents. That is no way to behave! Now see what you have done to the hero Vainamoinen! Come, before I tell your mother and complain to your father, remedy the mischief you have made."

The greybeard scolded Iron severely and then he spoke to the blood and ordered it to stop flowing.

"Stand like a wall, O Blood," he said, "like a bank that bounds the river. Stand still! You ought to know

67

enough to run quietly. Certainly, O Blood, it is pleasanter to move gently through the body than to rush
about wildly like this over the floor and across the
pebbled ground. You should know better, O Blood!"

He argued with the blood, he pleaded with it, he
warned it that if it did not stop flowing from Vainamoinen's knee, other enchantments would be used
against it: the blood would be boiled in a cauldron be-
longing to Hiisi, the Evil One! Finally the greybeard
called upon the Creator, Ukko himself, to press his
mighty hands upon the wound and close the gates
through which the red stream issued, and bar the path
of bleeding.

The blood heard him and ceased. The terrible flow
was stemmed.

Then the greybeard sent his son to the smithy to
prepare a healing ointment from the thousand-headed
yarrow and the sweet mountain-honey. The boy went
out and took the wild honey that drips from the
branches of the oak and he sought out strange grasses
such as grow in outlandish places, and he boiled them
in a pot for three long nights and three long days
until the magic ointment was nearly ready. Then he
added strange herbs gathered by nine wise men and
he boiled the mixture for three more nights and for
another three nights and yet another three nights.

Having done all this, he took an aspen branch and broke it off sharply. Then he smeared the tree with the magic salve, and the bough grew together and the tree was healthier than it was before. Still the boy was not satisfied. He took a stone that had cracked in two, and he rubbed both halves with the magic salve and the broken pieces of stone knit together to make a mighty rock. Now at last the boy was sure that the ointment could not be bettered, so he took it into the house and gave it into the hands of his old father.

The greybeard sniffed at it and tasted it, and declared that it was perfect. He took some of it between his fingers and rubbed it on Vainamoinen's knee, stroking him downward and stroking him upward, all the while praising the Creator who had put strength into his hands and words of healing into his mouth.

It was a painful business. Old Vainamoinen writhed and struggled under the burning touch of the magic salve and the hard hands of the greybeard.

Then the old man tore a piece of silk into strips to make a bandage, and wound it deftly about Vainamoinen's knee and around his foot, and spoke further words of healing, and with that Vainamoinen felt perfectly well again, indeed sounder and healthier than before. He had not a pain or an ache. His pains had been sent away to the Hill of Tortures and his

69

aches filled the stones on the Mountain of Suffering.
He could walk as he pleased and stamp his feet without hurt. He was full of joy and gratitude. He
thanked the greybeard, and especially he thanked the
Creator, without whose help he would never have
escaped whole and hearty from Iron's cruel work.

Then he yoked his chestnut horse to the sledge,
mounted the seat, cracked his beaded whip and drove
off in the direction of home. After all, the dazzling
girl was not meant for him. Her mother, old Louhi,
would marry her off to Ilmarinen, the smith, if he
forged her a magic Sampo. And besides, old Vainamoinen longed to see his own country again after all
his fearful adventures.

He drove for a day and for another day and for a
third day, and on the third day he reached the bridge-
head and saw the broad heaths of the Land of Heroes
stretching before him.

"Wolf!" cried old Vainamoinen, thinking of how
Joukahainen had wanted to drown him, "Wolf, go
seize that dreamer who told me I should never reach
home! Sickness, go devour that Lapp who said I
should never again walk among the sweet fields and
the broad heaths of my own country, the Land of
Heroes!"

But as he came nearer home, old Vainamoinen
70

shifted his cap on his head uneasily, for he was filled
with gloomy thoughts. He remembered that before
he had left the dark and misty regions of the North
Country he had promised to send thither his brother,
the great smith Ilmarinen, to forge a magic Sampo.
And old Vainamoinen was not at all sure that Ilmarinen would want to go.

But then he straightened his cap and began to sing.
As he sang there grew up a pine-tree, crowned with
flowers, and every needle on it was of gold. The
boughs rose into the air and reached the clouds and
touched the sky. Then the oldest magician sang a
shining moon onto the very top of the golden pine,
and he sang the stars of the Great Bear into its
branches. And in the back of his sledge he set the
golden pine that bore the false moon and the Great
Bear of his singing, and drove swiftly on.

Presently he came to a new-cleared field. Across
the field came a noise from the smithy and a great
clatter from the coal-shed, so old Vainamoinen knew
that he had indeed come home. He stopped his horse
and got down from his sledge and went to the forge to
find Ilmarinen.

And what happened when the two met, you shall
hear.

5

THE FORGING OF THE SAMPO

OLD Vainamoinen went at once to the smithy, where Ilmarinen was swinging his mighty hammer.

"Where have you been keeping yourself all this while?" asked the smith.

"I have been in the dark and misty Country of the North," answered old Vainamoinen, "traveling on snow-shoes in the company of famous sorcerers."

The smith laid down his hammer and looked at the oldest magician with interest.

"Tell me about your travels," he said. "What is it like in the North Country?"

"Oh, my friend and brother," answered old Vainamoinen, "there is something there worth traveling far to see. There is a girl there, as dazzling as the sun and as cold as the snow. She refuses every man who asks her in marriage, and makes mock of the greatest heroes. Half the folk of that region are forever speaking of her beauty; when one half stops the other half begins. Her face is as lovely as moonlight and even when she turns her back there is a brightness like the Starry Seven. You should see her, Ilmarinen! What is more, you, and you alone, have the chance to win her for your bride. You have only to forge a magic Sampo with its many-colored cover—a mere trifle for so great a smith as you are—and her mother will give her to you to be your wife forever."

"You are a sly one," answered the smith. "Perhaps you have already pledged me to her, so as to save your head and get your freedom. But as long as I live I am not going to those cold and misty regions. I have heard tales of the North Country. There the people eat each other. They even drown heroes."

"Nonsense," said old Vainamoinen. "It is a marvellous place. There is a pine-tree there with golden needles and a flowery summit. The moon shines on the tip of it and the Great Bear rests in the branches."

"I'll believe that when I see it with my own eyes," said the smith.

"So you shall," said old Vainamoinen quickly. "For I brought it home in my sledge to show you. It is standing on the edge of the corn-field right now."

At these words the smith put his hammer aside and

73

followed the oldest magician to the edge of the corn-
field, eager to see this marvel. There it stood, its
needles gleaming gold, the Great Bear tangled in the
branches and the moon shining from its tip. Ilmarinen
could not hide his amazement.

"Climb up, brother," said the oldest magician. "Go
and fetch down the moon, and the Great Bear too."

This would indeed be a trick, thought the smith,
and he began climbing up to the top of the golden
pine. But as he hoisted himself up the pine-tree began
to speak.

"Foolish fellow!" it said, laughing at him. "Do
you think, mighty as you are, that you can grasp the
reflection of the moon or take hold of false stars!"

At the same moment the oldest magician began to
sing. He sang a terrible tempest. He sang a wild wind.

"Oh, tempest," he cried, "carry the smith in your
boat! Wind, carry him in your skiff, far and far away
to the cold and misty regions of the North Country!"

And the storm, obedient to the oldest magician,
bore the smith Ilmarinen over the moon and under
the sun and on the shoulders of the Great Bear, till
he came to the North Country. There the storm set
him down, but not a dog barked at the sight of the
mighty smith.

74

The Forging of the Sampo

Old Louhi, the gap-toothed mistress of that place, came out to greet the stranger.

"Who are you," she asked, "who come in the path of the tempest, on the sledge of the wind? What hero may you be at whom even the watch-dogs do not bark?"

"No dog would dare bark at me," answered Ilmarinen.

"Tell me," said old Louhi then, "did you ever hear any stories of the mighty smith, Ilmarinen? Did you perhaps meet that great craftsman on your travels? We have been expecting him for a long time. He is supposed to come and forge a magic Sampo for us."

"I have heard tell of him," answered the smith. "In fact, I know him quite well. Indeed, I am Ilmarinen. I am that remarkable craftsman."

Old Louhi was delighted. She hurried back into the house and summoned her eldest daughter, the dazzling Maiden of the North Country.

"Come, my dear," she cried, "put on your finest dress and your brightest beads. See that your cheeks are rosy and smile your sweetest smile. For the great smith Ilmarinen has come, and he is going to forge us a magic Sampo."

Obediently the dazzling girl went to the store-room

75

and chose her finest dress and a girdle of copper and gold and ear-rings that jingled when she moved, and a silver head-dress. Then, rosy-cheeked and smiling, she came to meet Ilmarinen. Meanwhile old Louhi had taken him into the house and set a feast before him, with plenty of good drink too. But when the beautiful girl entered, he set down his goblet and pushed away his dish, and looked only at her.

"I am sure you can forge a magic Sampo for us," said old Louhi slyly. "And in return would you perhaps accept this charming girl as your bride?"

"It was I who forged the heavens," answered Ilmarinen promptly, "and who hammered out the vault of the air. Why shouldn't I forge a magic Sampo?"

He was ready to go to work at once. He had never seen such a great beauty as old Louhi's daughter, and he began to think that old Vainamoinen had done him no bad turn in sending him to the North Country. But he could not start his task because there was neither smithy nor furnace, neither bellows nor anvil, neither hammer nor mallet.

"Never mind," said Ilmarinen cheerfully. "Only old women despair. Only scamps leave a task unfinished. It is different with heroes."

And he looked about for a day and another day and yet a third day until he found a suitable place for a

76

smithy. He took a streaked stone and a great rock and built himself a forge, and he soon made a hammer and a pair of bellows, and heaped fuel for the furnace. For three days and three nights the servants were working the bellows. They worked so hard that they had to have boulders on their toes to keep them from toppling over.

At the end of the first day Ilmarinen stooped and stared into the furnace to see if something were shaping itself there. And indeed, there was a golden crossbow with a shaft of copper, tipped with silver. But the bow was of an evil disposition and demanded the right to kill a man every day and two men on feastdays, so the smith was ill-pleased and broke it to pieces and threw it back into the furnace. Once more all the servants bent to their task of working the bellows.

On the second day Ilmarinen stooped and looked into the furnace again. This time a red boat rose out of the flames, with copper oar-locks and a gilded prow. But beautiful though it was, the boat had an evil disposition. It insisted on sailing into war whether there was a quarrel or not. So Ilmarinen was angry at it and smashed it to splinters and threw them back into the furnace. Then he ordered all the servants to work the bellows mightily.

On the third day Ilmarinen stooped and gazed into

77

the furnace to see what might be forming there. This time he saw a heifer with the stars of the Great Bear on her forehead and the disc of the sun between her budding horns. But lovely as she looked, the little heifer had an evil disposition. She wanted nothing but to sleep in the forest and waste her milk on the ground. So Ilmarinen disliked her, and cut her into little pieces and threw the pieces back into the furnace, and set all the servants to working the bellows with more than half their strength.

On the fourth day he looked into the fire again and there was a plough with a golden share, a copper frame, and handles with silver mountings. But it had an evil disposition and insisted on ploughing up the corn-fields whenever it pleased. Ilmarinen was disgusted and broke it into fragments and threw them into the furnace.

But now the mighty smith knew what he must do. He sent the servants away, and he called the winds to work the bellows: the east wind and the wild west wind, the south wind and the blustering north wind. They blew for a day and another day and yet a third day. Fire flashed in the windows of the smithy. The sparks flew out of the door and rose to the sky. The smoke mingled with the clouds. Anyone but Ilmarinen would have been afraid of the flames that filled the furnace. But on the evening of the third day the mighty smith stooped and looked into the very bottom of the furnace and here he saw a strange, huge, wonderful thing. It was a magic Sampo, and the cover of it was of a thousand colors.

Ilmarinen took it and hammered it and welded it with many rapid blows, using all his skill and cunning, and when he was done, there stood the Sampo, with a corn-mill on one side and a salt-mill on another side and on the third side a coin-mill. There it was at last, finished and perfect, the many-colored cover turning round and round, the corn-mill grinding away, a chestful of meal for food and a second chestful for barter, and a third chestful for storage, while the salt-mill and the coin-mill worked as well. It was indeed a magic Sampo that could give corn-meal and salt and money enough and to spare.

The gap-toothed Mistress of the North Country, crafty old Louhi, could hardly wait to have it carried to the rocky hills, where it was set in the Copper Mountain and secured with nine strong locks. There it struck roots nine fathoms deep, one root in the earth, one root in the sand of the sea-shore and one root in the nearest mountain.

79

"Now," said Ilmarinen, "the Sampo has been forged. Will you give me your daughter to be my bride?"

But before old Louhi could reply, the dazzling girl spoke out:

"Here at home every summer has been sweet with the song of the cuckoo in the hedge and bright with the cranberries in the marsh. But if I go away, the cuckoo will forget to sing and the cranberries will not grow. Indeed, I do not want to be a wife so soon."

Ilmarinen pushed his cap sideways on his head. He was very unhappy. He saw plainly that he could not persuade the beautiful girl to leave her carefree life in her father's house. Not even her mother, old Louhi, would try to argue with her. He would have to go home without her.

So the old woman set meat and drink before the mighty smith, and feasted him well, and then she gave him a boat with a copper paddle, and called the north wind to blow him safely home to his own land.

He sailed for a day and another day and yet a third day over the cold blue sea, and on the third day he reached his own country.

Old Vainamoinen was there to greet him.

"Well," he cried, "and did you forge the Sampo, brother?"

80

The Forging of the Sampo

"Yes," answered Ilmarinen, with a heavy sigh. "I forged the magic Sampo, and a good job it was too. But the dazzling daughter of old Louhi would not come back with me, for all that."

"Never mind," said old Vainamoinen. "There are plenty of beautiful girls here at home who will be glad to marry such a mighty smith as you are."

But secretly old Vainamoinen was well pleased. Perhaps the dazzling girl still remembered her meeting with him, when he had had that misfortune with the axe. Perhaps she would not be sorry to see him again. If only he had a fine new boat to carry him back to the North Country!

He determined to build him a boat, but look where he would, he could not find suitable timber. Finally he summoned Sampsa, the little woodsman, and begged his help. Sampsa was glad to oblige the oldest magician, and went wandering eastward with his axe, that was handsomely inlaid with copper and gold, looking for proper timber.

Finally Sampsa came to an aspen three fathoms high. He was about to lay his axe to it when the aspen spoke.

"What do you want of me?" it asked.

"I want timber with which Vainamoinen, the famous singer, can build him a boat."

81

"I should make a leaky boat," said the aspen. "My branches are hollow. The grub has been at the heart of me three times this very summer."

On hearing this Sampsa turned and walked north. There he found a pine-tree that measured six fathoms. But when the pine-tree heard what was wanted, it said:

"Do not chop me down! I should never give you good timber for a boat. My wood is full of knots, and besides a raven has croaked in my branches three times this very summer."

So Sampsa turned about and walked southward. There he found a great oak, nine fathoms high. This time Sampsa asked the oak's permission before he raised his axe. At once the oak answered:

"Take me, indeed! My wood is well suited for old Vainamoinen's boat. It is not hollow. It has no knots in it. Three times this very summer the sun has worked magic in the heart of me and the moonlight has crowned me, and the cuckoos have given me health singing in my branches."

Then Sampsa smote the great oak and felled it and hewed the trunk in countless pieces for the boat of old Vainamoinen.

The oldest magician was delighted with the sturdy oaken timber. He sang himself a strong keel, and with

82

another song he built the broad sides, and with a third song he made the rudder and bound the rib-ends firmly and fixed the joints.

But when all this was done, there were yet three words lacking. Without them neither the prow nor the stern could be finished. Try as he might, he could not think of the three words.

Perhaps he could find them in the heads of the swallows or in the heads of the swans, or in those of the wild geese. But though he slaughtered flocks of wild geese, and flocks of swans, and many many swallows, and searched their brains for the words, it was all in vain. Then he said to himself he would be sure to find them on the tongues of the reindeer or in the mouths of the squirrels. But though he spread a whole field with reindeer and loaded benches high with squirrels, he could not discover the magic words on the tongue of any of them.

Finally, after deep thought, old Vainamoinen decided that they could only be found if he traveled to the dark kingdom of Manala, the Land of the Dead. So the dauntless old magician hastened off for the region governed by Tuoni, the Lord of the Dead. He walked for a whole week, pushing his way through thick shrubs, and for a second week through a place overgrown with bird-cherry, and for a third week through juniper bushes. And at the end of the third week he stood beside Tuoni's river, whose dark waters flow between the Land of the Living and the fearful Land of the Dead. And what happened after Vaina-moinen reached its banks, you shall hear.

6

THE SEARCH FOR THE THREE WORDS

OLD Vainamoinen stood on the shore of the dark river and shouted across to the dread island of Manala:

"Bring a boat, O daughter of Tuoni. Row this way, so that I may cross the river!"

The dwarfish daughter of Tuoni, Lord of the Dead, was kneeling on the other shore, washing her clothes, when she heard the old singer call her.

"You may have a boat," she called back, "if you tell me why you come to the Kingdom of the Dead, although you have not been conquered by sickness and no other fate has overcome you."

"It was Tuoni who dragged me here from my own country," answered the old singer.

"I know that you lie," said the dwarfish girl scornfully. "If Tuoni had dragged you here, he would be with you himself. The Lord of the Dead does not let people travel here alone. You would be wearing the hat of death on your head and the gloves of death would cover your hands. Tell the truth, Vainamoinen. What has brought you to Manala?"

"Iron has brought me to Manala," answered old Vainamoinen. "Strong steel has brought me to the Kingdom of the Dead."

"I know you are lying," said the dwarfish girl. "If iron had dragged you here, your clothes would be stained with blood. If strong steel had brought you, blood would be flowing from the wound. Tell the truth, Vainamoinen."

"It is water that brought me," answered the old singer. "The swollen waves of the sea have carried me to Manala."

"You are lying," replied the dwarfish girl. "If water had brought you here, it would be trickling from your clothes as it trickles from the clothes of the drowned. Tell me truly, and do not pretend any more: what has brought you to the Kingdom of Death?"

"It was fire," answered Vainamoinen. "Fierce flames have brought me to these shores."

"Indeed, you are a hopeless liar!" cried the dwarfish girl angrily. "If fire had brought you, your hair would be singed and frizzled, your beard would be

86

scorched and black. If you really want the boat to fetch you, Vainamoinen, you must tell me the truth. How is it you have come to Manala, though sickness has not overcome you and no other fate has conquered you?"

"Well," said old Vainamoinen, "it is a fact that I lied a little, but now I will tell the truth. I built me a boat with my singing. For a day and another day and a third day I shaped it by my magic songs. But on the third day, my shaft broke as I was singing, and so I have come to Manala to borrow a gimlet from Tuoni. Come ferry me across the river!"

"I never heard such nonsense," said Tuoni's daughter. "You have no reason to come to Manala. You are not even a little bit sick. You had best go home to your own country, and quickly too. Many come to these shores, but few return where they came from."

"That thought might frighten old women," said Vainamoinen proudly. "But no man, and certainly no hero, not the laziest of the lot, would be troubled by it for a moment. Bring the boat, daughter of Tuoni, and ferry me across the river. Indeed, I am tired of waiting."

"Woe to you, old Vainamoinen!" said the dwarfish girl, "who dare to come to Manala while you are yet alive." Nevertheless she left her washing, and took

87

the boat across the river and ferried the old singer to the other shore.

There he was met by her mother, the Mistress of the Dead. She greeted him as a guest and offered him a tankard of beer.

"Drink, old Vainamoinen!" said the Mistress of the Dead.

But sturdy old Vainamoinen first looked into the tankard and saw worms wriggling inside and frogs spawning at the bottom.

"Surely I have not come here to drink from Tuoni's tankards," he said. "Those who swallow this beer grow drunken and then perish."

"Then why have you come here?" asked the Mistress of the Dead.

At last old Vainamoinen told the real reason for his coming. He explained that when he was building his boat he found that he could not finish the stern or the prow without three magic words, and that he had not been able to find those words however far he traveled, so he sought to learn them from the dread Tuoni himself.

"Tuoni will never teach you his spells," answered the Mistress of the Dead. "Nor will you ever reach home again."

Old Vainamoinen did not want to believe this, but

he was very tired and made no answer. When the Mistress of the Dead invited him to a couch she had prepared, he was so weary that he lay down and at once fell asleep.

Now there was a witch-wife in the Kingdom of the Dead, an old crone with a sharp chin and a gift for spinning nets of copper wire and iron thread. Sitting on a rock among the waters she spun a thousand such nets in a single summer night. There was also a wizard, an old man with only three fingers, who was a skilful plaiter of nets. He sat on the same rock and in the same summer night he wove another thousand nets. Then Tuoni's son, who has crooked fingers hard as iron, took the nets and spread them crosswise and lengthwise across the river, so that old Vainamoinen should never be able to ferry back to the other shore, and never escape from the Kingdom of the Dead.

When Vainamoinen woke from his sleep he saw what had been done, and he reflected that unless he acted quickly he might have to remain in this wretched place for always and always. This would be an evil fate to befall the oldest magician. There was no help to be had from Tuoni. There was only misery in Manala.

So Vainamoinen turned himself into an otter swimming among the reed-beds, and then into a water-

snake wriggling in the muddy depths, and then into a
sly little adder crawling through the nets, and turning
and twisting he made his way safely through the
meshes and crossed the river to the other shore.

Early the next morning Tuoni's son, he of the
crooked fingers hard as iron, went out to examine the
nets. He found a hundred salmon-trout and small fish
by the thousand, but no sign of old Vainamoinen.

But though the oldest magician had escaped the
clutches of Tuoni, he had not found the three magic
words. Nor was anyone able to help him. At last one
fine day he met an aged shepherd who gave him
counsel.

"Have you never thought of seeking out the giant,
Antero Vipunen?" asked the shepherd. "There are a
hundred spells that are known to him alone. In his
vast mouth there are a thousand magic words. You
have to go down into his enormous belly and there you
will learn marvels. But it is not easy to get there. You
must go along a path leaping on the points of women's
needles, and over a cross-road paved with sharp swords,
and down a third road made of the blades of heroes'
axes."

"That journey will be no joke," said old Vainamoinen to himself. But he was determined to try it.
He would do anything to find the magic words and

"*He was fast asleep. A poplar-tree was growing from his shoulders and a birch-tree sprang from either side of his head.*"

finish his boat. His first move was to go to his brother Ilmarinen, the mighty smith, and ask him to forge iron shoes, iron gauntlets, an iron shirt, and a tough stake of iron, with a heart of steel overlaid with iron, so that he might make his way safely into the giant's belly. The smith only laughed at him, and said that Vipunen had perished long and long ago, and no magic words were to be learned from him any more. Nevertheless he consented to do the work, for which Vainamoinen paid him well.

Thus clad in iron and bearing his iron stake, the oldest magician stepped lightly over the path made of needles, and at the end of a day he came to the crossroads paved with sharp swords. He passed over it easily in a day, and at the end of a third day he had already made his way over the road made of the blades of heroes' axes, and reached the mouth of the enormous giant, Antero Vipunen.

Vipunen was far from dead, as the smith had said. On the contrary, he was very much live, and as full of magic as an egg of meat. But he was fast asleep. A poplar-tree was growing from his shoulders and a birch-tree sprang from either side of his head. At the tip of his chin stood an alder, and his beard was a willow-thicket. Great firs full of squirrels sprang from his brow and branching pine-trees grew

93

out of his teeth. This did not bother old Vainamoinen. He whipped his sword out of its scabbard and swiftly hacked away all those thick trees. Then he thrust his iron stake between Vipunen's huge jaws.

"Wake up, you lazy giant!" cried the oldest magician. "You have been sleeping long enough beneath the earth."

Suddenly Vipunen woke up. He did not care for this rough treatment. He bit the iron stake but he could not break it. Old Vainamoinen was standing just over the giant's mouth. As the giant gripped the stake between his teeth, Vainamoinen's foot slipped, the giant opened his jaws wide, and Vainamoinen tumbled into his mouth. The giant gulped him down with a shout.

"I am a great eater," he said. "I have eaten ewes and goats and barren heifers. I have consumed swine in plenty. But I never had a dinner like this. I have never had such a tasty morsel."

But poor old Vainamoinen did not rejoice.

"Now indeed I am in a bad way," he said to himself, "prisoned here in the stable of the Evil One. What shall I do?"

Then it occurred to him that he had a knife in his belt with a haft of maple-wood, and of this he fashioned a little boat and rowed back and forth among the giant's innards, rowing through the narrow channels of his body and exploring every passage. But these journeys did not trouble the giant Vipunen, they merely tickled him.

Then old Vainamoinen decided to take other measures. He took off his iron clothing and made himself a smithy of his shirt and bellows of his sleeves, using the fur for a wind-bag, and he made an air-pipe of his trousers and an opening of his stockings. He used his knee for an anvil and his own elbow for a hammer. And thus he began to work as a smith. There in the stomach of the giant Vipunen he began to hammer. He hammered for a whole night without resting and for a whole day without stopping.

"What sort of man is this?" the giant asked himself, as he felt the hammering in his insides. "What hero may this be? I have swallowed a hundred heroes, and gulped down a thousand men, but I never swallowed anything like this. He has filled my mouth with coals and set firebrands on my tongue; he has even thrust iron slag into my throat. Go wander elsewhere, stranger," roared the giant, "get out of here! Hurry, before I go to find your mother and tell her how badly you are behaving. It would make the poor old woman very sad to hear it. She would grieve to think that her son should be so wicked.

"Of course," the giant went on, thoughtfully, "it

95

may be that you are a sickness sent by the Creator to work my death. Or perhaps you are a strange sort of creature altogether, bribed by wicked folk and hired to torment me. Whence have you come to bite me and worry me and gnaw at my guiltless belly? From the realm of mighty wizards or from the home of evil spirits or from the region of the dead?

"Pest of the earth, leave my poor belly alone! Stop gnawing at my liver, leave off biting my spleen, don't attack my lungs and my loins! Stop hacking at my spine! If you don't leave me in peace I shall call all the heroes to help me, poor weak man that I am! Yes," the giant bellowed, "I'll call on the Mistress of the Earth and the Mother of Waters, and even Ukko, the Creator himself. Go on home like the wicked thing you are, and let the lightning announce you. Go and break the gate-posts and knock people's heads together, and drive the men into a corner and twist the women's heads, go push the horses out of the stable and make the cattle cross-eyed with fear. Go back where you came from, wherever that evil place may be!"

The giant went on grumbling and growling and naming all the possible and impossible places to which he wanted to send old Vainamoinen. But for all the giant said, the oldest magician answered simply:

"I find it very pleasant down here. I prefer to stay

where I am. Your liver is very nourishing. I can make a good meal of your lungs. Your fat is delicious. In fact, I think I shall plunge my smithy a little deeper in your belly and strike my hammer a little harder."

The giant bellowed more loudly than ever.

"Perhaps," said old Vainamoinen slyly, "I shall think better of it if you teach me your magic spells. You know a thousand of them and I want to learn them all, every word."

Then the giant Vipunen, who had all the magic of the world in his mouth and boundless power in his breast, began at once to sing his ancient songs. He knew songs that no child has ever heard and that even the mightiest heroes do not understand. He sang all of them in order, the story of the beginning of the beginning, when the Creator parted the air from the water, and of the creation of the lights of heaven. The sun listened to his songs and the moon waited to hear them. The waves stood still while he sang and the furious waterfall was silent. But none listened so eagerly or so carefully as old Vainamoinen, down in the giant's belly. When he had heard every spell, he bade Vipunen open his jaws wide and promised to crawl out.

"I have eaten and drunk all manner of things," said the giant Vipunen then. "I have swallowed a

97

thousand dainties, but I never tasted anything like you, old Vainamoinen. You were a most delicious morsel. It was good when you came, but it is still better that you are going."

At that he opened his great jaws wide and stretched his gigantic mouth, and old Vainamoinen journeyed out of the monstrous belly and slipped out of the great mouth of Vipunen, and leaped over the open heath like a squirrel, making his way swiftly home.

"Tell me," said his brother the smith, when he saw him, "have you found the words you needed to fashion the stern and the prow of your boat?"

"Indeed, yes," answered old Vainamoinen, and with the help of Vipunen's magic, rapidly and deftly he completed his boat.

He painted it red, and gilded the prow and overlaid it with silver, and very early the next morning he pushed it out into the water. Then he hoisted a red sail and a blue sail, and steered out into the sea. Not wanting to row, he called upon the wind to blow him toward the dark and misty region of the North Country. For he was still thinking that he might win the dazzling girl to be his wife. And what happened on that journey, you shall hear.

7

THE TWO SUITORS

IT WAS early morning when old Vainamoinen set out in his red boat with the blue and red sails. But he was not the first to rise that day. His lovely sister, Annikki, had wakened before daybreak and gone down to the shore to wash her clothes. She had rinsed them and wrung them out and spread them to dry, and now she stood up and looked over the sunlit water. She was surprised to see a blue speck far out among the waves. At first she thought it was a flock of wild geese, and then she mistook it for a shoal of fish, and then she thought it must be a stump riding on the billows. But finally she saw that it was the blue sail on the vessel of old Vainamoinen. She hailed him and asked him where he was going.

"Salmon-fishing," he called back. "The salmon-trout are spawning up the river."

"Don't tell me such a silly lie," said his sister. "I

have often seen my father and my grandfather before him go out to capture the salmon. There were always nets in the boat, and a heap of tackle, and beating-poles. You have nothing of the sort. Where are you going?"

"I am going after wild geese. They are flying over the sound looking for food."

"I know you are lying," said Annikki. "I have seen my father and my grandfather before him go out after wild geese. They carried tight-strung bows and had their hunting-dogs with them. You have no such thing. Tell the truth, Vainamoinen: where are you going?"

"Into battle," answered the old singer. "When a mighty fight is raging I cannot sit home quietly: I must join the other heroes and give blow for blow."

"Do you think I don't know what it means to go into battle?" cried Annikki. "When my father went to fight with other heroes he had a hundred men rowing with him, and a thousand men standing in the boat, and swords heaped under the seats. Tell me honestly, Vainamoinen: where are you going?"

"Well," said the old singer, "it is true I lied a little. But now I will tell you the truth. I am going to the dark and misty Country of the North, where people eat men and they even drown heroes. But that does not

100

matter to me, for I am going to fetch the dazzling Maiden of the North Country to be my bride."

When Annikki heard this she gathered her skirts in her hand, and letting her wash lie, she ran as fast as she could to the smithy. There she found her brother Ilmarinen, the mighty smith. He was hammering away at an iron bench with silver trimmings, and his shoulders were covered with ashes from the furnace and his head was black with soot.

"Brother," said Annikki breathlessly, "if you make me a fine shuttle and some golden ear-rings and some girdles with links of silver, I will tell you something you ought to know."

"I will do all that," answered Ilmarinen, "if your news is important. But if it isn't, I'll feed the furnace with your trinkets."

Annikki shook her head and laughed.

"Tell me, Ilmarinen," she said, "are you still thinking of that girl up in the North Country—the one who was promised to you as a reward for forging the magic Sampo?"

Annikki knew very well that the smith had been thinking of nothing else for the past two years.

"While you are welding and hammering," she went on, "making horse-shoes all day and working at your sledge all night, so that you may journey to fetch your

101

bride, someone cleverer than you is speeding there ahead of you. I have just seen Vainamoinen in a boat with a gilded prow and a copper rudder sailing for that cold and misty land."

At this news Ilmarinen let his hammer drop to the floor of the smithy.

"Annikki," he promised, "I will make you the finest shuttle. I will forge you rings for your fingers and two or three pairs of golden ear-rings and five or six girdles with links of silver. But you must do a favor for me, too, little sister. Go to the bath-house and kindle a fire of small chips there and see that the stones are properly hot, so that I can have a steam-bath. Fetch me some soap too, for I must wash off the coal-dust of a whole autumn's labor, and the soot of a whole winter's work."

At once Annikki ran and got some branches broken by the wind and burned them, and gathered stones from the river and heated them, and cheerfully fetched water from the holy well, and warmed the bath-whisks on the hot stones, and then she mixed milk and ashes and marrow-fat to make a fine soap. And all the while that she was preparing the bath-house, Ilmarinen worked at the trinkets he had promised her.

When Annikki came to tell him that the bath was

ready, he gave her the rings and the ear-rings and the girdles and a splendid head-dress as well, and marched off to the bath-house. He scrubbed himself and he rubbed himself, he cleaned himself and he steamed himself. He washed his eyes till they sparkled and his face till it shone. He washed the soot from his neck till it was white as a hen's egg, and his body till it glistened. Then Annikki brought him a linen shirt and well-fitting trousers and fine stockings that his mother had woven when she was a girl. She brought him boots of Saxon make, and a blue coat with a liver-colored lining, and a woollen overcoat tailored in the latest fashion, with splendid fur to top it. She fastened a gold-embroidered belt around his waist, and gave him brightly colored gloves, and a handsome high-crowned hat that his father had worn as a bridegroom. Ilmarinen looked splendid indeed.

As soon as he was dressed in these rich clothes he told his servant to harness the chestnut stallion and yoke him to the sledge, and fetch six golden cuckoos to sit on the frame and seven blue birds to perch on the reins and sing. If he appeared in this splendor, heralded by singing birds, surely he would delight the dazzling girl and she would consent to be his bride. Then he called for a bearskin to sit on and a walrus-hide to throw over the sledge.

103

When the servant had provided him with all these things, Ilmarinen begged the Creator to send a fine snowfall so that his sledge might glide swiftly over the drifts. The Creator obliged him at once: the heath was soon covered with snow, and the berry bushes were white with it.

Ilmarinen cracked his whip and drove off, praying for luck. He drove for a day and another day and a third day, and on the third day, as his gay sledge went clattering along the shore, he overtook old Vainamoinen.

The smith hailed the old singer out on the waters, and Vainamoinen waited to hear what he had to say.

"Let us make a friendly compact," said Ilmarinen. "We are both setting out to win the dazzling girl for a bride. But let us agree that neither of us will seize her by force, and that neither of us will marry her against her will."

"I agree," said old Vainamoinen. "Let the girl be given to the husband of her choice, and there will be no quarrel between us." He was sure that she would choose that famous singer, that great hero, the oldest magician, the glorious Vainamoinen. As for Ilmarinen, he was sure that she would choose the mighty smith, the forger of the heavens, the welder of the magic Sampo, the handsome Ilmarinen.

104

The Two Suitors

So they traveled on, each by the path he had chosen. The boat sailed so fast that the shore echoed with the noise of its speed. The horse ran so swiftly that the earth resounded with the clatter of the swaying sledge.

Before long there was loud barking in the cold and misty region of the North Country. The grizzled house-dog bayed and wagged his tail to announce that strangers were nearing.

"Go, daughter," said the Master of the North Country, "find out what the house-dog is barking about."

"I have no time, father," said the girl. "I must clean the big cow-shed and grind the corn between the heavy mill-stones, and then I must sift the flour."

The Master of the North Country turned to his wife, gap-toothed old Louhi.

"Go, old woman," he said, "and see why the house-dog is making that racket."

"I have no time," said old Louhi. "I must prepare dinner. I have an enormous loaf to bake, but first I must knead the dough."

"Women are always in a hurry, and girls are always busy toasting themselves before the stove or lying in bed," complained the old man. "Go, my son," he said, "and see what the matter is."

"I have no time," said the youth. "I must sharpen

105

the hatchet, and there is a great pile of wood that I have to cut up into faggots."

All this while the dog was out in the furthest corn-field, wagging his tail briskly and yelping without pause.

"He isn't barking for nothing," said the old Master of the North Country. "He doesn't growl at fir-trees."

So he went to find out for himself. When he reached the corn-field he saw a red boat sailing out in the bay and a gay sledge driving along the shore. The old man hurried home to his wife.

"There are strangers coming. I wonder what it means."

"We shall soon know," said crafty old Louhi. She called the little serving-maid to lay a log on the fire.

"If the log sweats blood, the strangers mean trouble, but if it oozes water, their errand is a peaceful one."

The gentle little serving-maid hastened to place the choicest log on the fire. It did not sweat blood, neither did it ooze water, but instead honey trickled from it and fell in golden drops on the hearth.

"Aha!" said old Louhi, delighted. "Those strangers must be noble suitors." And she hurried out into the court-yard. There she could see the red boat with the gilded prow coming towards the shore, and a hero handling the copper rudder. She saw too the gay

106

sledge, with six golden cuckoos perched on the frame and seven blue birds on the reins, all singing at once, and a hero holding the reins.

Old Louhi turned to her daughter, the dazzling Maiden of the North Country.

"Which of these heroes will you choose for a husband?" she asked. "That is old Vainamoinen in the red boat. You remember the famous singer: he is bringing a cargo of treasure. In the sledge sits Ilmarinen, the smith, but he comes empty-handed. Go fetch a tankard of mead and hand it to the hero of your choice. Hand it to old Vainamoinen," she advised her daughter. "He is the wisest of all heroes. Besides, his boat is loaded with treasure."

"I do not care for treasure," answered the dazzling girl, "nor for a wise man who is old. I will marry a young man, with bright eyes and strong hands, a man like the skilful smith, Ilmarinen, who forged the magic Sampo."

"You do not want to marry a smith, my lamb," said crafty old Louhi. "You will have to scrub his sooty aprons. When you are his wife you will have to wash his sooty head."

"I don't care," said the dazzling girl. "I don't want old Vainamoinen. An old husband is a nuisance."

Just then old Vainamoinen steered his boat into the

107

harbor and stepped out and came to the house. He was no sooner within than he reminded the dazzling girl of her promise to marry him, if he would make her a splendid boat out of the splinters of her spindle and the fragments of her shuttle.

"But have you built such a boat?" she asked.

"Yes, truly have I!" answered old Vainamoinen. "A noble ship strong to face the storms and light as a leaf on the waves."

"Oh, what do I care for seamen!" cried the dazzling girl. "As soon as it blows up they want to set sail, and if the wind is in the east, they frown and are gloomy. I do not want to marry a man who thinks only of ships."

Before old Vainamoinen could answer her, his brother the smith entered the house. The dazzling girl greeted Ilmarinen with a smile and handed him a great beaker of mead. But Ilmarinen did not taste it.

"I will not put my lips to the drink before me," he said, "until I am granted the bride for whose sake I forged the magic Sampo, and for whom I have been longing these two years."

"That is all very well," said old Louhi slyly, "you may have my daughter for your bride, but there is one task I must ask you to perform first. There is a field full of vipers that must be ploughed. It has not been touched since the Evil One, Hiisi, ploughed it long and long ago."

Ilmarinen did not know how this was to be done, and sought counsel of the dazzling girl. She told him to forge himself a coat of mail and iron shoes and a plough ornamented with silver and gold, and he would have no trouble in subduing the field of vipers. The smith took her advice, clad himself in steel and iron, hammered out the gold and silver for a great plough, and went to the open field. It was a fearsome place, thick with writhing serpents, but Ilmarinen spoke to them persuasively, and advised them to get out of the way of his sharp ploughshare. It was not long before they all slipped off and out of sight. Then he ploughed the field and came to tell old Louhi that the task was accomplished and to ask for his bride.

"You may have her," said the gap-toothed Mistress of the North Country, "if you catch the Bear and the Wolf that live in the forest of Tuoni, Lord of the Dead. Bring them to me muzzled and bridled, and the girl is yours." Crafty old Louhi knew very well that hundreds of heroes had gone on this errand, but none had ever come back.

"It will be easy for you," said the dazzling girl, when the smith told her of this second task. "You have only to sit on a rock where the spray of the waterfall sprinkles you, and there forge a muzzle of the hardest steel and an iron bit. Neither Tuoni's Bear nor his fierce Wolf can escape you then."

So Ilmarinen stood on a rock in the midst of the stream and in the spray of the waterfall forged himself what was needed. Then, with the steel muzzle in one hand and the iron bit in the other, he went to seek the beasts of Tuoni in the depths of the forest. He prayed to the Daughter of the Clouds to blind the animals with a mist so that they could not see him coming, and there in the dread forest of Tuoni he crept up on them and muzzled them with the magic bits and brought them both back to old Louhi.

"Here is the great Bear of Tuoni, and his Wolf as well. Now give me your daughter," said Ilmarinen.

"I will give you my darling," answered old Louhi, "as soon as you bring me the Pike that swims in Tuoni's River. It is fat and scaly, and it must be caught without a net, nor dare you grasp it with your hand." The old woman knew that hundreds of heroes had gone to catch Tuoni's Pike, but not one had returned from that adventure.

A third time the smith asked the maiden to help him. He could not imagine how the Pike was to be caught without using net or tackle.

110

"Be of good cheer, Ilmarinen," said the dazzling girl. "Forge yourself a fiery eagle, with talons of iron and claws of steel and wings like the sides of a boat. He will dive into the River of the Dead, and bring up Tuoni's terrible Pike."

So the smith went once more to the forge and forged a bird of fire and flame, as the maiden had directed. Mounted on its wings, that were broad as the sides of a boat, he flew towards the dread river. The eagle was so huge that one great wing swept the sky and the other trailed the water. His iron talons dipped into the river and he whetted his flaming beak on the cliffs. He carried Ilmarinen swiftly to the shore of Tuoni's stream, and there the two waited for the Pike to rise out of its muddy depths.

But instead of the Pike, a wicked water-sprite rose out of the river and snatched at Ilmarinen. It would have dragged him down, but the eagle took the wicked creature by the neck and nearly twisted its head off and sent it down to the black muddy bottom.

Then the Pike of Tuoni rose slowly to the surface. He was no ordinary fish. He had a tongue as long as two axe-shafts and teeth like those of a rake. His gorge was as wide as three great rivers and his back was the length of seven boats. He opened his awful

111

jaws and tried to seize Ilmarinen between his terrible teeth.

But the eagle was not a small bird either. His beak was a hundred fathoms long, and his tongue the length of six spears, and each of his iron talons was like five scythes. He rushed upon the Pike and struck at it fiercely. But the Pike pulled at the eagle's broad wings and tried to drag him under the water. Up the eagle soared into the air. He hovered there a moment and then he dived. He struck one savage talon into the Pike's terrific shoulders, and gave himself a purchase by fixing the other talon firmly in the rocky cliff. But he did not thrust it deep enough and his talon slipped from the rock, and the Pike slid away and dived into the water. The shoulder of the fish was almost cloven in two and his sides were scored with the marks of the eagle's steely claws, but he had escaped the great bird's clutches.

Now the furious eagle, with fiery eyes and flaming wings, swooped a third time, seized the monstrous Pike in his talons and dragged him out of the water. Then what a battle took place between the huge bird and the terrible fish! The air glittered with iron splinters. The river heaved like a sea of steel. There was a gnashing and a thrashing, as the giant struggle continued. Finally the eagle made a mighty thrust

"Now the furious eagle, with fiery eyes and flaming wings, swooped a third time, seized the monstrous Pike in his talons and dragged him out of the water."

and flapping his broad wings he bore the Pike off in triumph to the top of a tall pine-tree. There he ripped open the belly of the fish and tore the head from the neck and began to feast.

"Wicked eagle!" cried Ilmarinen in anger. "Why are you so greedy? You have destroyed the Pike that I was to carry back to old Louhi!"

But the eagle, having satisfied his hunger, soared off into the heavens, breaking the horns of the moon in his flight.

Then Ilmarinen took the head of the terrible Pike and carried it back to old Louhi.

"Here is a present for you," he said. "You can make a chair out of the bones in this head that will remain forever in the lofty halls of your house."

The gap-toothed Mistress of the North Country did not thank him too graciously. She did not care that he had brought only the head of the Pike, the bones of which would truly make a noble chair, but she was angry because he had performed every task she had set him, and now she would have to give him her beautiful daughter.

As for old Vainamoinen, he was the saddest of all.

"A man should marry when he is young," he said gloomily, "and choose his life's companion early. It it a grief to be old and have no wife and no children."

115

But Ilmarinen and the dazzling girl were full of joy, and eager for the preparations for the wedding. And how the feast was arranged, and what guests were invited, and how the bride and groom fared, you shall hear.

8

THE WEDDING-FEAST

NOW there were great preparations in the North Country for the wedding of old Louhi's beautiful daughter and the smith Ilmarinen. The feast was not made ready in a day or a week. The guests would be many, great eaters and strong drinkers, and it was needful to provide fish and flesh and cakes and ale in plenty.

Old Louhi was not one to let her guests want for anything. So she sent for the fat ox of Carelia to be sure of enough meat. This was no ordinary ox. While he switched his tail over one river, he stooped his head over another. His horns were so long that a swallow could fly for a whole day without resting before he passed from one tip to the other. His back was so huge that a squirrel could run for a whole month to cover the space between his neck and his hinder-end. Old Louhi sent a host of men to pull at his horns and another host to drag at his muzzle before she could get the fat ox to the fields of the North Country. It was not easy to find a butcher. But when the fat ox was slaughtered, he yielded a hundred barrels of meat and more than a hundred of sausage, and six casks of fat, and from his blood they got seven boat-loads of rich gravy.

Then old Louhi began brewing ale of hops and barley and sweet honey from far places. So much wood was needed to heat the kettles that for miles about the islands were left bare of trees. So much water was used that the lakes shrank. Under the giant vats the fires burned for many weeks, till folk in distant places wondered at the smoke that filled the sky. The kettles were singing, the stew-pans were hissing, the large loaves were baking in the oven, and the red ale was foaming.

Meanwhile the men had not been idle. They had built a great hall to house the banqueters. It was so high that if a cock stood on the chimney and crowed, those beneath never knew it. It was so long that if a dog stood at one end of it and barked, those at the door never heard him.

Now the hall was built, and the bread was baked, and the meat was roasted, and the beer was stored safely in the oaken casks with copper taps. The red ale

118

was crying out indignantly from the barrels for someone to come and praise it.

"If you do not soon find a famous singer to come and taste me and tell my fame," shouted the ale, "I will burst the hoops of the casks and trickle out on the ground!"

So old Louhi called her little serving-maid to journey forth and summon the folk from near and far to the wedding-feast she had prepared. She bade the maid invite the poor and the needy, bring the cripples in sledges and the lame on horseback and the blind in row-boats. And she sent for old Vainamoinen, the famous singer, to sing the wedding-songs and to praise the red ale. All the people of the North Country and all the folk of the Land of Heroes were invited to the wedding.

Only one young man was not asked, the lively Lemminkainen, because he was a quarrelsome fellow who might make trouble and spoil the feast. But his doings are another story.

The little serving-maid went in six different directions and on eight different roads, asking all the people of the North Country and all the folk of the Land of Heroes, the neediest householders and the poorest beggars as well, to come to the wedding.

Meanwhile old Louhi, the Mistress of the North

Country, was busy indoors and out. One fine day, when she was in the midst of her many tasks, she heard a great noise, the cracking of whips and the rattling of sledges. She turned her gaze toward the north. Then she looked sunward, shading her eyes with her hand, to see what she could see, for the noise was terrifying.

"Unhappy woman that I am!" she cried. "What army is this I hear, coming to destroy me?" And she went further, to observe more closely.

But it was no army moving against her, it was the great host of guests coming to the wedding, and among them the bridegroom, with six golden song-birds on the shafts of his sledge and seven blue-birds perched on the reins, all singing together. Then Louhi bade her servants unharness the bridegroom's horse, and lead him to the spring where water gushed forth like sweet milk, and give him fodder of choicest barley and boiled wheat mixed with pounded rye out of a golden bowl, and stable him softly and curry him with a fine comb of walrus-bone, and cover him with a cloth embroidered in gold and silver.

Ilmarinen, the bridegroom, was so tall and broad, and the wedding-gifts were so many, that they had to remove the door-posts and raise up the cross-beams of the roof and widen the walls of the house and shift

120

"The guests drank until their beards were white with the foam."

the floor-planks so that he might enter easily, and so that room might be found for the fine presents he had brought with him. They took his hat and his gloves politely, and they led him to the highest seat against the blue-painted wall, facing the red boards of the table, and all the folk shouted with joy.

Then old Louhi feasted her guests nobly. She brought them the best butter and an abundance of cream cakes. The table was loaded with heaped plates of salmon and pork. And all were served well, but Ilmarinen, the bridegroom, was served first. Then the great hooped tankards were handed round filled with foaming ale, and all the guests drank till their beards were white with the foam, but the bridegroom's beard was whitest of all. Finally the ale came to old Vaina-moinen, the famous singer, and he lifted his tankard and called out to the red ale.

"Delicious ale!" he cried, "you shall make us shout. You shall make us sing with golden mouths. Who will chant us a wedding-song? The benches do not sing and the floors do not talk, and the windows and the tables and the chimney are all silent unless the folk who sit on the benches and feast at the tables are merry."

There was a small thin boy sitting on the floor.

"I am only a little boy," he said. "And my stomach

123

is not round yet, but if the stout men will not sing, then, thin as I am, I will whistle, so that the evening may be cheerful."

"It is not fit for a child to sing," said an old man who sat by the stove. "We want no weak piping. And the songs of girls are foolish. Let the wisest among us sing in a tuneful voice, and all will rejoice to hear him."

Now the wisest among them was of course Vainamoinen, the famous singer, so he lifted his voice and sang and spoke and sang again for their pleasure, till the women were all laughing and the men in high good humor.

"Small is my wisdom and poor is my song," he said when he was finished. "But if the Creator were to sing His songs to you, He would sing the sea to honey and the gravel to fat peas and the mountains to cakes. He would sing the cow-sheds full of cattle and the wasteland full of wheatfields. He would sing our host into a coat of lynx-skin and our hostess into a rich gown, and her daughters into embroidered boots and her sons into red shirts. Grant Your blessing upon us all, O Creator, and upon our feast here. Let the ale stream in rivers and the mead flow in torrents. Bless our host at the head of the table and our hostess in her storeroom and their sons casting the fish-nets, and their

124

daughters at their weaving. They have feasted us well, and when the banquet is over, may they rejoice for a whole year!"

But at last the eating and drinking and singing came to an end, and it was time to prepare the bride for her departure. At first she wept to leave her father's house, and there were those who warned her that she would never again be as carefree as she had been in her girlhood. But one wise old woman told the bride that she had nothing to fear if she behaved well in her husband's house.

"You must obey your husband's mother and honor your husband's father," said the old woman. "Rise at cock-crow to tend the sheep and the cattle and the pigs. And do not look sloppy in the early morning either, for your husband will not like it. Wash the children of the household, even those not your own, and give them a bit of bread so they do not rouse the others with their crying. Sweep the floor and wipe the windows with a damp duster. Scrape the stove and brush the rafters. Fetch the water and bake the bread and scour the meal-tubs. Heat the stones in the bath-house and fill it with steam for your husband's father. Do not sing too loudly at your work, and do not groan when you turn the handmill: leave the groaning to the handmill. When it is time to spin and weave, ask ad-

125

vice of your husband's mother, not of strangers in the village. And when guests come, give them hearty welcome. And above all, always speak well of your new relations, no matter how they treat you.

"Alas," said the old woman. "I who tell you this did not behave so. When I was a young wife I was lazy and careless and selfish. I thought only of how homesick I was, and I said evil things of my new relations. I made my husband so angry that he beat me. And so I ran away from home. But my mother was dead and my father was dead, and my brother treated me like a stranger and his wife treated me like a beggar. Do not do as I did, but follow my advice, and your marriage will be a happy one."

Only one thing the wise old woman did not know. She did not know that Ilmarinen's bride, beautiful as she was, had an unkind heart.

Then an old man spoke to Ilmarinen and bade him treat his young wife well.

"Give her wheaten bread to eat and well-brewed ale to drink. Do not let your mother whip her. Do not let your father scold her. Do not let the neighbors blame her. But if she does not behave properly, then you must beat her. Do not do it in the meadow, or the neighbors' wives will hear the quarrel and gossip about it. You must beat her in the house. And do not give

126

her a black eye, or your father will see it and wonder.
You must strike her on the shoulders. Take my advice. I had a bad wife, and I spoiled her. But once I
gave her a beating, and after that she was as good as
gold."

Only one thing the old man did not know. He did
not know that fair as the bride was, she had a cruel
nature.

When the old man had finished talking, the bride
began to cry. The thought of leaving her mother and
father and going to a strange house seemed dreadful
to her. But Ilmarinen comforted her and promised to
make her happy in her new home, and then he lifted
her into his sledge and carried her off. He drove for a
day and another day and a third day, holding the reins
in one hand and embracing his bride with the other.
And on the third day they reached the house of
Ilmarinen, the smith.

Now the folk at home had been expecting the bride
and groom for so long that the eyes of the old people
at the windows were teary with watching, and the feet
of the children who waited outside were frozen with
standing, and the people walking up and down the
shore were spoiling their shoes. When the young
couple finally arrived, Ilmarinen's mother came out to
welcome the bride, and to tell her that all the folk of

127

the household, and the cow and the foal and the lamb as well, were impatient to greet her, and that the very threshold of the house was asking for her to cross it, and the door-handles were calling for her fingers to turn them. The old woman was full of praise for the beauty of the bride, since she could not see into her unkind heart, and full of praise for the furs and blankets and hand-woven cloth that she had brought.

Then they made a feast for the bridal-party, roast meat in handsome red dishes, and salmon cut with golden knives, and cakes with big lumps of butter, and so much spicy ale that the lips of all were foaming with it. Lusty old Vainamoinen was there also to sing songs of welcome, and praise those who had prepared the feast. Then he sang of the dazzling bride and of Ilmarinen, the handsome bridegroom, and he praised all the guests too, those who were young and pretty, and those who were old and stately. But at last his songs came to an end and he got into his sledge and drove off.

So the feast of welcome ended, and the time came for Ilmarinen's young wife to take up her duties in her new home. Now among the servants there was a new-comer, a slave-boy named Kullervo. And how Kullervo was treated by the smith's wife and how he rewarded her, you shall hear.

128

9

THE SLAVE'S REVENGE

KULLERVO had yellow hair and handsome blue stockings, but he was a sullen fellow. Before he was born there had been a bitter feud between his father and his uncle. His father had been killed, and he had grown up in his uncle's house, where he was treated like a slave. He hated his uncle, and whatever task was given him, Kullervo did the wrong way. When they set him to rock the baby to sleep, he destroyed the baby's cradle. When they sent him to clear the forest, he spoiled the best timber. When they bade him build a fence around the field, he built it without an opening so that no one could enter the field. His uncle determined to be rid of him, and sold him to Ilmarinen, the smith. In exchange for Kullervo, the smith gave two battered kettles, three broken hooks, five dull scythes and six old rakes. Satisfied that he had made a good bargain, Ilmarinen took the wretched boy home with him.

Early in the morning Kullervo went to the smith's young wife and asked her what work she had for him to do.

Ilmarinen's wife looked at Kullervo and thought that a boy with such handsome yellow hair and such fine blue stockings should be good for something.

"I will tell you what to do," she said. "You shall be a herd-boy and go and tend the cattle at pasture."

But then she looked at his sullen face and she took a dislike to Kullervo. Now it must not be forgotten that though Ilmarinen's young wife was of dazzling beauty, she had an ugly nature. She was the daughter of old Louhi, the crafty Mistress of the North Country, and like her mother, she was full of malice. She decided to play the slave-boy a mean trick.

She baked a great cake of oat-flour and wheaten too, and she spread it with butter and laid fat bacon on the crust, but in the middle she placed a stone. This cake she gave to Kullervo for his supper in the field.

"Do not eat the food I give you," she said, "until you have driven the herd to pasture. Take my milch-kine to the open meadows and let them graze, and guard them carefully. Dig wells for them on either

130

side of the pasture, so that they may drink. And bring
them home again with full udders."

Then she called a blessing down on the herd from
all the gods of the woods and meadows and streams,
and from Ukko the Creator himself, to keep them safe
from the creatures of the wilds, and to make them
sleek and plump and fill their udders with sweet rich
milk. And she sent them off in charge of Kullervo.

The herd-boy put his cake in his wallet and drove
the cows along the marshes and over the heath. He
was very miserable.

"What sort of life is this I must lead," he muttered
to himself, "watching the calves and following the
tails of the cows!"

So he lamented his sad lot, wandering over the
meadows, while Ilmarinen's young wife sat com-
fortably at home, enjoying hot soup and cakes spread
with the freshest butter in the barrel.

The day drew on toward evening and Kullervo decided that it was time for him to rest and eat. So he
sat down on a green hillock and took out of his wallet
the cake that the smith's wife had given him. He
turned it round in his hands and looked at it, but he
did not bite into it. He thought it strange that the cake
was so heavy.

131

"Many a cake has a smooth crust," said Kullervo to himself, "but the dough is nothing but chaff." And he made up his mind that before he took a mouthful he would see what it was like inside. He took out his knife, the only thing in the world that was precious to him, because it had belonged to his father, and tried to cut the cake. The blade struck against the stone, and the point of the knife broke.

Kullervo was furious to think that his precious heirloom was broken. He wanted to revenge himself on the smith's wife, but he did not know how.

There was an old crow perched on a bush nearby.

"You can have vengeance, orphan boy," cawed the crow hoarsely. "Drive the cattle into the marshes and let the wolves and the bears devour them. Then call the bears and the wolves together and change them into cows. Lead them home to the smith's wife as though it were the cattle you were bringing back. That will be a pretty vengeance for the loss of your only treasure."

On hearing this advice from the crow, Kullervo jumped up and plucked a twig of juniper for a switch and drove the cows into the marshes and the oxen into the thicket to be eaten by the bears and wolves.

"Just wait, you wicked woman!" he cried. "I am weeping for my father's knife, my one and only treasure, that is broken because of you. But soon you will weep for your cattle!"

Then he sang the wolves and bears into the likeness of cows and oxen, and drove them back to the farm-yard.

In the swamp on the way he found a cow-horn, and as he drew near the house he lifted the horn to his lips and blew a loud blast upon it.

"Praise be to the Creator, the herd has come at last!" said the smith's wife when she heard the horn. She had been waiting impatiently for her milk and her summer butter. "But wherever did you get that horn?" she asked, as Kullervo came towards her. "You blew such a blast on it that my ear-drums are bursting and my head aches."

"I found the horn in the swamp," answered Kullervo sullenly. "The cows are standing in the shed now," he added, "waiting to be milked."

"Will you go and tend the cows?" the smith's young wife called to her mother-in-law. "I have not finished kneading my dough."

"The thrifty housewife goes to milk her cows first of all," said Kullervo.

The smith's wife did not like being reproved by the slave-boy, and without further words she went to the shed.

133

"Oh, how beautiful the herd looks!" she cried, when she saw it. "How sleek the cows are, and what full udders they have!"

Then she sat down on the stool, drew the pail toward her and started to milk. She gave a tug at the udder, and a second tug, and a third tug, but no milk came. Instead, the cow before her changed back into its real shape of a wolf, and the other cattle turned into wolves and bears too.

"You wicked cowherd!" cried the smith's wife, "to drive wild beasts into the farmyard!"

"You wicked woman!" answered Kullervo grimly, "to give me a stone for bread! I broke my knife on it: the knife of my dead father, the only precious thing in the world to me!"

Even as he spoke, the beasts sprang upon the smith's wife and began clawing at her fiercely.

"Forgive me!" she screamed. "Forgive me, and recall your magic spells or I shall die!"

"Die, then," said Kullervo harshly. "There is room enough for you in Tuoni's kingdom."

And in spite of all her shrieks and prayers, the smith's wife was torn to pieces by the wild beasts there in her own farmyard.

Kullervo did not stay to find out what Ilmarinen would do when he learned that his wife had met such a dreadful death. Satisfied with his revenge, the herd-boy rushed away. But an evil fate pursued him. At last the day came, when, full of remorse for his wicked deeds, he asked his sharp sword if it would slay him.

"I have drunk the blood of the innocent," answered the sword. "Why should I not drink the blood of the guilty?"

So Kullervo set the haft of the sword firmly in the ground, and turned the point against his breast and threw himself upon it, and so perished.

In due time the news of Kullervo's death came to the ears of wise old Vainamoinen.

"Friends," said the wisest magician then, "be sure you do not rear a child crookedly, for a child crookedly reared will never grow straight, nor get understanding. Though he lives to be old, he will never have the mind of a man and the thoughts of a hero."

As for Ilmarinen the smith, he was filled with sorrow over the loss of his wife. She had paid dearly for her cruel treatment of Kullervo, and poor Ilmarinen had to pay for it too with loneliness and grief. He mourned her in the evening when he came home to his lonely house. He wept for her through sleepless nights. He fasted for days on end, bewailing her. For a

135

whole month he did not swing his hammer. For two months he wept, and for three he lamented.

But when the fourth month came, Ilmarinen put aside his grief and went to the lake to gather silver and gold. And what he did with it, you shall hear.

10

THE GOLDEN IMAGE

WHEN Ilmarinen had as much gold and silver as he needed for his purpose, he collected a great pile of wood. He had wood enough to load thirty sledges. This he burned to charcoal for his smithy. Then he took the gold and silver and put them in the furnaces until they were red-hot. His servants stood with naked shoulders, working the bellows in the fiery smithy, while Ilmarinen tended the furnace. He had decided that he could no longer do without a wife, so he was fashioning a new one for himself out of silver and gold.

But the servants did not press hard enough on the bellows, so Ilmarinen took hold of them and worked them himself. Then he bent down and looked into the furnace. There he saw a ewe with fleece of copper, silver and gold.

"Others may admire you," said Ilmarinen, "but

137

you are no wife for me." And so he set to work again.

A second time he looked into the furnace and there was a foal with a golden mane and a silver head and a copper tail.

"Others may find pleasure in you," said Ilmarinen, "but you will not make me a wife." And he worked the bellows more powerfully than before.

The third time he looked into the furnace he saw a maiden with a face of silver and golden hair and a glittering form. Others might not have liked her, but Ilmarinen was delighted with her. He worked hard to fashion her hands and feet. But the feet would not support her and the arms would not embrace him. He made ears, but they did not hear, and eyes, but they did not smile, and a tender mouth, but it did not speak to him.

"What a lovely girl she would be," said Ilmarinen, "if only she had sense and knew how to talk!"

He took her gently out of the furnace and laid her down on a silken couch, while he warmed the bath-house. He prepared three tubs of steaming water and brought bath-whisks and soap, and washed away the furnace ashes that clung to the golden maiden, and washed the soot from himself too.

She was indeed beautiful, but when Ilmarinen embraced her, the metal made him so cold that he called for several blankets and two or three bearskins and five or six woollen mantles. It was no use, whichever side he turned to her became as icy as a frozen lake.

"This is not so pleasant for me," said the smith. "I will take the golden maiden to Vainamoinen. He has no wife. She will do for him nicely."

No sooner said than done.

"Look, Vainamoinen," said the smith. "See the lovely girl I have brought you. Isn't she beautiful? Her mouth is just the right size, and her chin isn't too broad either."

Lusty old Vainamoinen looked at the golden image in amazement.

"What have you brought this golden witch to me for?" he asked.

"Why, with the best will in the world," answered the smith. "I brought her to be your wife, to rest on your knee and nestle in your arms."

"My dearest brother," said old Vainamoinen, "I suggest that you throw this girl into the furnace and forge all sorts of trinkets from her. Or else take her off to Russia, or carry her to the Saxons who marry the spoils they win in battle. But it really doesn't suit my position to have a wife of silver and gold."

Then Vainamoinen turned to the young people who were gathered about him.

139

"However poor you may be," he said to them, "when you are grown-up heroes, do not marry a woman of gold or make yourselves miserable for the sake of silver. The breath of silver freezes and gold is the coldest of metals."

"You are right, brother," said Ilmarinen with a sigh, and he cast the golden image aside.

Then he yoked his horse, mounted his sledge, and drove off.

Now it occurred to Ilmarinen that he might get a new wife where he had got the first one. True, old Louhi's daughter had had nothing to recommend her but her great beauty. She had been selfish and cruel. But the smith thought that among old Louhi's other daughters there must be one who was both beautiful and good. At all events he was determined to try. So off he drove to the North Country.

He drove for a day and for another day and for a third day, and on the third day he came to the broad courtyard of old Louhi's homestead. The old woman came out to meet him, and at once began inquiring after the health of her daughter.

"Is she well? Is she content?" asked old Louhi. "And how does she get on with your mother? And what does her father-in-law think of her?"

The dismayed Ilmarinen bowed his head so that his

cap fell sideways. He did not tell old Louhi the whole grim story of Kullervo's revenge; he only said that his wife had been carried off to the dark Kingdom of Tuoni, Lord of the Dead, and that he had come to ask for old Louhi's second daughter to cheer his loneliness.

Old Louhi wailed with pain and rage at the news.

"Not another child of mine shall you have, you sooty smith!" she cried. "I would sooner give my second daughter to the raging whirlpool and the teeth of Tuoni's pike than to you!"

Ilmarinen pursed his lips and shook his head angrily at these harsh words. He pushed his way into the room where old Louhi's second daughter was sitting and spoke to her himself. He pleaded with her to come home with him and take her dead sister's place in his household, to bake his bread for him and brew his ale, and be a good wife to him.

But the girl called him a scoundrel, declaring that he had murdered her sister.

"Perhaps you will kill me too," she said. "I want a better husband than you will make. I want a finer house than the black coal-house of a smith."

This made Ilmarinen so angry that he seized the girl and rushed from the room like a snowstorm, pushed her into his sledge, and drove off.

The girl wept and moaned, but all in vain. Ilma-

141

rinen held her fast, guiding the horse with one hand and grasping her with the other.

"If you do not release me," the girl warned him, "I will smash your sledge to pieces."

"This sledge was fashioned by a strong smith," answered Ilmarinen. "The boards are bound with iron. You can struggle and push as hard as you like, you will not even scratch my sledge."

"Let me go," cried the girl, "or I will turn into a lake-fish and swim away like a herring."

"Then I will turn into a pike and swim after you," said Ilmarinen.

The girl turned and twisted and almost broke her fingers struggling to free herself, but Ilmarinen held her fast.

"If you do not release me," she cried, "I will turn into an ermine and hide among the rocks of the forest."

"Then I will turn into an otter and run after you," replied the smith.

"Let me go," begged the girl, "or I will turn into a lark and fly up behind a cloud in the sky."

"You shall not escape that way," said Ilmarinen. "I will turn into an eagle and swoop down on you."

Old Louhi's second daughter saw that it was no use. She could not move the stubborn smith from his purpose. And though she knew that many a hero won his wife by capture, she was not reconciled.

She lifted her head and looked out and noticed fresh footprints on the snow.

"What has crossed our path?" she asked.

"A hare," said the smith.

"He is handsomer than you are," the girl taunted the smith, "with his cleft mouth and his crooked legs."

Then they saw the tracks of a fox and next the footprints of a wolf, and each time the girl cried out that she preferred the companionship of the wild beasts to that of the smith.

Ilmarinen bit his lip and did not answer. He had made up his mind to have old Louhi's second daughter for his wife. A hero often won his wife by capture. And in the end all would be well. He held her firmly and drove on.

It was nightfall when the sledge rattled into a village. Ilmarinen was tired out with the long journey and the trouble of holding the reins with one hand and the girl with the other. He was glad to halt and rest awhile. He no sooner lay down than he fell fast asleep.

But the daughter of crafty old Louhi did not sleep. Instead she made merry with a stranger in the house.

143

Indeed, she liked him so well that she was quite ready to take him for a husband.

When Ilmarinen woke up and found that the girl whom he planned to make his wife wanted to marry a stranger, he was filled with jealousy. Not all her taunts and struggles had made him so angry as to know that she preferred another husband to himself.

"I will not sing her into a wild creature," he said to himself. "A girl like that would only trouble the forest. Nor will I turn her into a water creature: the fishes would have nothing to do with her. I had better take my sword to her."

But when his sword heard this, it reproved the smith sternly.

"I was not made to kill women," said the sword. "I was not wrought to hurt the weak."

"You are right," said Ilmarinen. "I will change her into a sea-mew. She can do her screaming on the cliffs, and moan on the jutting headlands, and if she wants to struggle, she can struggle with the winds."

So he began to sing, and with his singing he cast a spell upon old Louhi's second daughter, and she turned into a sea-mew.

This was all very well, but Ilmarinen was still without a wife, and he was very much depressed. Sorrow-

" 'He is handsomer than you are,' the girl taunted the smith, 'with his cleft mouth and his crooked legs.' "

fully he got into his sledge, and with bowed head he drove back toward his own country.

When he reached home, lusty old Vainamoinen came out on the road to meet him.

"What is the matter, brother?" asked the famous singer. "Why are you in such a gloomy mood? Why do you wear your cap pushed sideways on your head?"

At first the smith did not answer.

"Tell me, brother," said old Vainamoinen, "what has become of the wife you went to fetch? Where did you leave her? Why are you returning home alone?"

"She was no wife for me," answered Ilmarinen. "I turned her into a sea-mew. Now she is screaming and moaning on the cliffs. I don't want her."

"So that is the way of it," said old Vainamoinen. "But tell me, how do they fare in the North Country?"

"Finely," said Ilmarinen. "And why shouldn't they fare well there? Have you forgotten that I forged them the magic Sampo that grinds corn and salt and money, as much as anyone could want? They lead a rich life there, ploughing and sowing. They never lack for abundant crops."

Lusty old Vainamoinen scratched his head thoughtfully.

"They have the magic Sampo that you forged for

147

them, brother," he said, "and you have not even a wife! Things are going ill with us. What do you say that we make a journey together to the North Country and seize the magic Sampo with its many-colored lid?"

"We can't very well do that," answered the smith, though the idea pleased him. "They have carried off the magic Sampo to a hill of copper and there it lies hidden. It is fastened with nine locks, and three roots have sprouted from it, each of them nine fathoms deep. One root is firm in the earth, the second is fixed in the sand of the seashore, and the third plunges in the heart of the hill where the Sampo is hidden."

"Nevertheless, we shall be able to carry it off," insisted lusty old Vainamoinen. He knew that such an expedition would distract his brother, the smith, from his troubles. And in the end, Ilmarinen was persuaded.

And how they traveled to seize the Sampo, and what adventures befel them, you shall hear.

11

THE HEROES MEET
LEMMINKAINEN

FIRST of all the two brothers discussed the best way to travel, by land or by sea. Ilmarinen argued that if they went by sea, a storm might blow up, the wind might drive them out of their course, and they might even lose their oars and have to row with their fingers. Vainamoinen agreed, but he could not help thinking how pleasant it was to go by water, and much less wearisome.

"If you prefer, we shall go by land," he said. "But in any case you must first forge me a new sword with a sharp edge, so that I can fight the wild beasts and chase off the wild people of the North Country, where they eat men and it is said they even drown heroes."

So the smith Ilmarinen went to his forge and cast iron and steel and silver and gold on the glowing charcoal, and set his servants to work the bellows, till the iron spread out like soup and the steel was as soft as dough and the silver shone like water and the gold swelled up like billows. Then he constructed a fine sword with a golden hilt, and worked at the blade and inlaid it with precious metals and ornamented it richly. A moon shone on one side of it and a sun on the other, and stars gleamed on the haft. He carved a neighing horse on the tip and a mewing cat on the knob and a barking dog on the sheath. It was a splendid sword.

Vainamoinen was delighted with it. He took it up and brandished it and with one stroke he clove open an iron mountain. It was a very good sword indeed.

Then Ilmarinen set about fashioning a strong suit of armor for himself. At last they were both ready and the time was come for departure. They took their yellow-maned horse, a one-year-old foal, and bridled it, and set out for the North Country, to fetch the magic Sampo.

They drove swiftly along the shore, and they had not gone far when they heard a strange sound. It was a bitter lament, and seemed to come from the harbor.

"Is that a girl crying?" asked old Vainamoinen. "Let us go and see what the trouble is."

So they went in the direction of the sad sound. But no girl did they see. Instead they saw a ship riding in

150

the harbor, crying as though its heart would break.

"What are you crying for, O ship?" asked old Vainamoinen. "Are you crying because you are clumsy? Or are you having a bad dream as you lie at your moorings?"

"A boat longs for the sea," answered the ship between sobs. "Its tarry sides long for the water as a girl longs to be a wife in the house of her husband. I am crying because I want to set sail. When I was built, they said I would be a war-ship and carry home the spoils of battle. But I have never once been in a fight. I have never been filled with plunder. Other boats, even bad ones, sail into battle and come home loaded with treasure. But although I am sturdily built, here I lie at my moorings, rotting away, with the worst worms in the country gnawing at my timber, and the birds building nests in my masts and the toads of the wood leaping about my decks. It would be better for me if I were a pine on the mountain or a fir-tree on the heath with a squirrel in my branches and a puppy playing under my boughs!" And the ship began to weep afresh.

"Do not cry, O ship," said Vainamoinen gently. "Do not fret any more. Soon you shall go into battle. Soon you shall feel the billows of the open sea washing your sides."

151

At this the ship stopped crying, and began to be cheered.

"But tell me," said old Vainamoinen, "are you as fit to bear us into battle as you are beautiful to look upon?"

"Indeed, yes," answered the vessel. "My decks are spacious. My sides are strong. I could carry a hundred rowers. A thousand men might stand amid-ships."

On hearing this, old Vainamoinen began to sing. He sang handsome young men with smoothly brushed hair and strong hands and well-booted feet on one side of the ship, and on the other side he sang girls with glittering head-dresses and copper belts and rings on their fingers. He sang till the ship's benches were filled with people, some old men, but mostly youths and maidens. Then he seated himself in the stern, and Ilmarinen came aboard too, and old Vainamoinen bade the ship speed onward to the North Country, floating as lightly as a water-lily on the waves of the sea.

First he set the young men rowing while the girls rested, but the ship did not move. Then he bade the young men lay aside the oars, and the maidens row, but still the ship did not stir. Then the old folk took up the oars, while the young people watched. They wielded the oars till their heads were shaking, but the ship did not budge. Then Ilmarinen, the mighty smith, sat at the bench and set to rowing. Now indeed the ship began to move steadily and quickly, and the splash of the oars and the noise of the rudder was heard in the far distance. Ilmarinen rowed so mightily that the oar-locks hissed like geese, and the oars croaked like ravens, and the planks trembled. And old Vainamoinen sat in the stern, steering the red ship onward.

They had not sailed far before they came to a cliff with a wretched village at its foot. Here lived Lemminkainen, whose many adventures are a story all by themselves.

He was leading a wretched existence on this lonely promontory. The grain would not grow on this shore. The fish would not come to his nets. He was hungry and sad. There he sat, mourning his evil fortune, and looking out over the water. Suddenly he noticed a rainbow and a little cloud beyond it. But soon he saw that it was not a rainbow and not a little cloud, but a red ship, filled with handsome men and maidens, with a noble fellow rowing and a hero in the stern steering.

Lemminkainen lifted his voice and shouted over the water with all his might.

"Whose ship is this coming over the sea?"

153

"Don't you know the hero at the oars?" called the men and women on the ship. "Don't you know the noble steersman?"

"But of course: it is Ilmarinen the smith, and Vainamoinen the famous singer," he cried, as they came nearer. "Where are you going?"

So they told him that they were on their way to the North Country to seize the magic Sampo. This news pleased Lemminkainen mightily. Here was an adventure that he wanted to share. He begged Vainamoinen to take him along.

"I have a good sword. I have strong hands and powerful shoulders. Make me one of your company."

Old Vainamoinen thought that the young man might give them good help in combat. But before promising to take him along he first asked politely what the stranger's name was, and of what race he came.

"My name is Lemminkainen," answered the young man. "Your brother the smith knows me. But if I were to tell you my story it would take more than one night and perhaps two days as well."

Now the famous singer loved nothing so much as a story. He did not care how long it was, if only it was full of adventures. And he thought it would do the company no harm to rest awhile before continuing

154

their difficult journey. So he beached the red ship, and all the folk gathered to hear Lemminkainen's wonderful tale. And you too shall hear it, before you hear how the quest for the Sampo ended.

Though Lemminkainen was still young and strong, he had already passed through many adventures.

When he first came to manhood he was a gay fellow who liked fooling and fighting. He was so handsome and merry that he had only to look at a girl for her to fall in love with him. But he did not want to marry any of the girls on the island where he had his home. The bride he wanted lived in far-off Saari, and her name was Kylliki. She was of noble birth, and so lovely that she was called the Flower of Saari.

Kylliki had had many suitors, but she had refused them all.

When Lemminkainen told his mother that he was going to woo Kylliki, his mother said the proud beauty would never have him.

"She comes of a noble house," said his old mother. "You should not try to marry above your station."

"My humble birth does not matter," answered Lemminkainen. "She will take me for my good looks."

And in spite of his mother's warnings, he harnessed

155

his stallion, mounted his sledge, and drove off to Saari. He was in such a hurry that when he came clattering up to Kylliki's gateway, his sledge overturned and he fell out. All the girls laughed to see him tumble onto the road.

Lemminkainen did not like to be laughed at. He made up his mind that they would pay for their mockery. He engaged himself as a herd, and spent his days in the meadows with the cattle and his nights dancing as always. Soon all the girls of Saari were in love with the handsome youth. But though he danced with each one in turn, his heart was set upon Kylliki.

One fine evening, not a month after his arrival, the girls were dancing together on the heath near a little grove. Kylliki was there too, the most graceful of them all. Suddenly who should come driving up to the dancing-space but Lemminkainen, his swift horse harnessed to his sledge. This time he did not tumble out. He leaned from his sledge, snatched up Kylliki from among her companions, cracked his whip-lash, and drove off with her. Now it was his turn to laugh.

"Keep this a secret!" he called to the girls over his shoulder, "or I will sing all your sweethearts off to the wars and you will never hear of them again!"

Poor Kylliki wept and sobbed and begged Lemminkainen to set her free. When he would not listen, she threatened him with the vengeance of her five strong brothers and the seven strong sons of her uncle. But Lemminkainen paid no attention.

"Unhappy girl that I am!" cried Kylliki. "I, who was so gently reared, to be forced to marry a worthless fellow, a rude quarrelsome churl!"

But Lemminkainen spoke to her tenderly and promised to cherish her always, to take her to a kind house, where there was great plenty of everything needful.

"And if I am not of noble birth," he said, "I have a noble sword, no man living has a better."

At this Kylliki, who was beginning to be comforted, sighed sadly.

"If you want me to love you," she said, "and be a good wife to you, promise me that you will forget that sword of yours. Swear to me that you will not be lured into battle, for the sake of silver or of gold."

Lemminkainen was so glad to have won Kylliki that he promised readily.

"But you must promise me something, too," he said. "Never go out in the evening to dance with the village girls." For he thought this did not befit a married woman, and besides, he wanted to keep

157

Kylliki all to himself. She was quite willing to satisfy Lemminkainen on this score, and so they pledged their troth.

He brought her home, and his mother was full of praise for his beautiful bride, the Flower of Saari.

For a while the young couple lived contentedly enough. The lively Lemminkainen did not go forth to battle, and the lovely Kylliki stayed away from the village dances.

But one morning early Lemminkainen went out to fish. He was gone all day and when night came he had not returned. Kylliki did not like being left alone. She forgot her promise and went off to the village to join the girls at their dances. It was not long before Lemminkainen learned of what she had done. He was enraged. If she could break her promise, why should he keep his?

"Mother!" he cried, "wash my shirt in the venom of the black snake, and dry it quickly so that I may wear it in battle. I am going to the North Country to fight."

All his mother's pleas were in vain. He was bound to go, and when he had fought the young men, he declared, and won fame as a warrior, he would find a maiden who would love and honor and obey him, and who would make a happy home for him.

158

The Heroes Meet Lemminkainen

"But you already have a wife," said Lemminkainen's mother.

"Kylliki is no wife of mine," he stormed. "Let her go to all the dances and sleep where she likes. I do not want to see her any more."

His mother warned him of the sorcerers he would meet in the North Country, and of their wicked enchantments, but Lemminkainen said he had met sorcerers before this and conquered them with magic of his own, singing them into the whirlpools of Tuoni's dark river, where they were asleep forever. With this Lemminkainen turned away, and unconcernedly began to brush his hair.

Still his mother, afraid of what might befall him, tried to hold him back, but this only made the stubborn Lemminkainen angrier than before. In his fury he flung his hair-brush at the stove, and the comb after it.

"When you see that brush running with blood and blood dripping from the comb, then you may know that harm has come to Lemminkainen!" he cried. "My armor is magic enough against magicians. My sharp sword is sufficient enchantment for me."

Then he harnessed his fiery horse to his sledge, cracked his whip, and was off for the North Country. The silver sand scattered under his sledge-runners. The golden heather crackled as he passed.

159

He drove for a day and for another day and for a third day, and on the third day he came to a homestead. At once Lemminkainen stopped the mouth of the watch-dog at the gate with a magic spell, so that none should be warned of his coming. Then he stood outside of the house and listened.

He heard many people talking within. The sound of music came through the walls. The sound of singing came through the shutters. Lemminkainen stepped up softly and looked in. The house was full of wizards. Singers crowded the benches. Musicians sat along the walls. Beside the hearth sat a Northern sorcerer, making songs of Hiisi, the Evil One, in a hoarse voice.

Lemminkainen thrust boldly into the room.

"A song is good when it is finished," he said. "The shortest verses are the finest, and the greatest wisdom is unspoken."

Now the house he had entered was that of old Louhi herself, the crafty Mistress of the North Country. She was angry at these rude words of the stranger.

"We have a watch-dog," said she, "who loves to bite bones. He is a great licker-up of fresh blood. How is it that he never warned us of your coming?

160

And who are you who push thus boldly into the house, without a dog to lift his voice against you?"

"I have not come without a store of magic," replied Lemminkainen. "Many the songs my mother taught me, many the songs that I know."

And with eyes shining like flame, and fire flashing from his furred cloak, the lively Lemminkainen began to sing. He sang the best singer in the house to silence. He filled the mouths of the wizards with pebbles. He piled rocks over the cleverest magicians, and sang the sorcerers from their benches onto the treeless plains and away from the hearthstone into roaring whirlpools. He sang the young warriors weaponless and the strong men helpless. Only one man he spared, a wretched cowherd, old and blind and mean-hearted.

"You have banished the young men and the old men," said the cowherd. "Why have you left only me?"

"You were not worth banishing," said the lively Lemminkainen. "You do not know any spells now, old and blind as you are. You were always the worst of cowherds and now you are of no account."

The blind herdsman was deeply angered by these words, but he made no answer. He slipped quickly out

161

of the door and made for the open country, and hid himself by the dread River of Tuoni, Lord of the Dead. There he bided his time, lying in wait for Lemminkainen.

Satisfied that the wizards were banished, the lively Lemminkainen now bethought him of his errand. He turned to old Louhi and asked for her tallest, fairest daughter in marriage.

"Indeed, no," said the Mistress of the North Country. "You have a wife already."

"Kylliki is no wife of mine now," said Lemminkainen. "All she can think of is to go dancing with the girls of the village. I want a better wife than that."

"Well," said crafty old Louhi, "if you really want a wife, I may perhaps give you my daughter. But first you must prove worthy of her. First you must go out and capture the elk of Hiisi."

Lemminkainen was ready enough to undertake this task. And how he performed it, and what followed after, you shall hear.

12

THE TRIALS OF
LEMMINKAINEN

LEMMINKAINEN pointed his javelin, sharpened the bone tips of his arrows, and strung
his bow with strong sinew. But he could not hunt the
elk of Hiisi without snow-shoes.

So he commanded a smith famous for this work to
fashion him a pair of splendid snow-shoes. The smith
spent a whole autumn shaping the left shoe and a
whole winter carving the right shoe. He fixed the
frames and fitted the rings, and lined the frames with
otter-skin and the rings with the skin of the red fox.
Then he smeared the runners well with grease made
of reindeer fat.

Lemminkainen tried the shoes and they fitted perfectly. He bound his quiver on his back, flung his bow
over his shoulder, grasped his pole firmly, and pushed
forward, first on his left shoe, then on his right.

"There is not a four-footed creature running," he cried, "who can escape Lemminkainen on his snow-shoes."

And he started off.

But his boast was heard by Hiisi, the Evil One, and Hiisi at once set about making the task hard for Lemminkainen.

He formed a magic elk, using willow branches for the horns and the bark of the pine for the back. He shaped ears of the leaves of the water-lily and the eyes were water-lily flowers. Then Hiisi spoke to the elk and bade it run to the breeding-place of the reindeer, to the grassy plains of the North Country.

"Run fast!" said Hiisi. "Run till the men who follow you are sweating with the chase. Above all, run from Lemminkainen!"

At once Hiisi's elk rushed away, past the barns and over the plains. He ran so fast that he kicked over the tubs in the houses and upset the kettles on the fire, and the meat was thrown out and the soup spilt in the cinders. Then the children began to laugh and the women began to cry and the dogs began to bark and the old people grumbled.

Lemminkainen chased the elk, gliding over the marshes till sparks flew from his snow-shoes and smoke rose from his staff with the speed of his going.

164

The Trials of Lemminkainen

He traveled over hill and dale, and finally he came to the far end of the North Country. There he heard the dogs barking and the children laughing and the women crying and the old people complaining. He asked what all the commotion was about.

"It is all because of the elk of Hiisi, the Evil One," they told him. "He charged in here and kicked over the tubs and upset the kettles and spilt all our dinners into the ashes."

Lively Lemminkainen struck his left snow-shoe into a drift and pushed his pine-wood staff forward like a living serpent and glided swiftly away.

"Let the men come and help me bring the elk home," he shouted as he went. "Let the women wash the kettles and set all the children to gathering firewood. You will need all your pots to cook the elk's meat after I capture him."

He speeded forward so fast that at the first stride he could no longer be heard and at the second stride he could no longer be seen and at the third stride he had leapt up to Hiisi's elk. Lemminkainen promptly threw a collar of birch-wood about his neck and tethered him to a maple pole in an oaken pen. Then he stroked the elk's back and patted him gently on the belly.

"I should like to rest here awhile," said Lemminkainen, thoughtfully, well content that he had caught the elk. "It is very pleasant here. If only I had a pretty girl to keep me company!"

At that the elk grew furious.

"Can you think of nothing but pretty girls?" cried the creature. "What sort of fellow are you, anyway!"

In his fury he tore away from his tether and broke out of the pen and went rushing wildly over the plains and marshes till he could no longer be seen.

Lemminkainen was vexed. He chased after the elk, but in his haste he plunged his left snow-shoe into a hole and it broke, and the frame of his right snow-shoe was dashed to pieces against the ground. He did not know where to turn.

He thought for a long while as to whether he should give up the chase and go home, or whether he should try once more. Finally he decided to ask the favor of the god who ruled the forest and begged the nymphs of the wood to turn the game in his direction, driving the quarry straight into the hands of the hunter. The forest deities were pleased by his words and listened graciously to his prayers. Then with powerful enchantments he mended his broken snow-shoes and glided forward through the depths of the woods.

For a whole week he traveled, singing as he went. His songs delighted the wood-nymphs, and they lured

168

Hiisi's elk from his lair and drove him over the tree-covered hills and delivered him up to Lemminkainen. The hunter threw his lasso over the creature's neck and stroked its back. Then, having rewarded his helpers, he journeyed swiftly to old Louhi's homestead and claimed her daughter for his bride.

But crafty old Louhi said that first Lemminkainen must perform another task. He must bring back to her the wild horse of Hiisi.

Lemminkainen thought this could not be any more difficult than capturing Hiisi's elk. Forth he went with a golden bridle slung over his shoulder and a silver bit in his hand, and after traveling for a day and another day and a third day he caught sight of Hiisi's wild horse. Fiery sparks flew from its mane and smoke issued from its nostrils. But with the help of Ukko the Creator, and with wise words of magic, Lemminkainen bitted the wild steed and bridled it, and mounted on its back, he went riding gaily back to old Louhi to claim her daughter for his bride.

Again crafty old Louhi put him off. She would give him her daughter, said she, only when he had brought back to her the swan that swam on the river of Tuoni, Lord of the Dead.

This was the most dangerous task that Lemminkainen had been asked to perform. But he was willing

169

enough to attempt it if only he could win the wife he sought. So he took his cross-bow and hurried to the banks of the dread river of Tuoni, Lord of the Dead.

Now Lemminkainen knew what risks he ran in undertaking this task. But one danger he did not know. He had forgotten the slight he had put upon the blind cowherd when he had banished all the wizards and paid no heed to him. But the cowherd had not forgotten. Lemminkainen thought no more of the insulting words he had spoken to the blind herdsman. But the herdsman had not forgotten them. At the turn of the murky river of Tuoni the blind herd lay in wait for Lemminkainen, to do him injury.

The cowherd had the keen hearing of the blind, and when Lemminkainen, bow in hand, approached the turn of Tuoni's dreadful river, the herdsman recognized his tread at once. With a cry of vengeance he summoned from the foaming cataract a serpent, and bade it strike Lemminkainen in the arm-pit and the shoulder, and plunge its venom through his heart and his liver.

Against this hurt all Lemminkainen's spells were useless. He was stricken unto death. Then the blind cowherd seized the young man and threw him into the midst of Tuoni's whirlpool. The bloodstained son of Tuoni, Lord of the Dead, caught him on his sword-point and hacked him into five pieces and hewed him into eight fragments, and sent them floating down Tuoni's dark river.

Now every morning and every evening that Lemminkainen had been absent, his old mother, remembering his parting words, had looked at his brush and his comb, for if they were as before, then she knew her son was safe. But on this evening she saw blood flowing from the comb and red drops oozing from the brush. So she knew that mortal hurt had come to Lemminkainen. Weeping and lamenting, she set out at once for the North Country, to discover what had befallen her son.

At last she came to the house of crafty old Louhi.

"Where is my son?" asked Lemminkainen's mother. "Where is he who is my silver staff and my golden apple?"

"Perhaps he has been eaten by a wolf. Maybe he has been devoured by a bear," said old Louhi.

"My son could crush a wolf between his fingers. He could master a bear without any weapon," said the old mother. "Tell me the truth."

Finally old Louhi said that Lemminkainen had gone to fetch the swan from Tuoni's river, but she did not know why he had never returned.

Sadly the old mother turned her steps in the direc-

171

tion of Tuoni's dark river, asking of all whom she met whether they had seen Lemminkainen. The oak-tree answered that it had troubles of its own, for it was always being chopped up for faggots. The path said that it could not fret for any but itself, for it was always being trampled by heavy feet. The moon only sighed over its own lonely journey through the sky. Then the old mother asked the sun:

"Have you seen my Lemminkainen? Have you seen him who is my golden apple and my staff of silver?"

And the sun told her what had happened. At once Lemminkainen's mother went to Ilmarinen the smith, and begged him to forge her a mighty rake, with steel teeth a hundred fathoms long and a copper handle of five hundred fathoms. With this she would rake the dread river of Tuoni. And she prayed the sun to shine with all his strength that the sultry heat might put to sleep the evil race of Tuoni, Lord of the Dead. The smith forged the rake for her, and the sun shone so fiercely that all the wicked warriors of the Kingdom of Death fell into a deep slumber.

The old mother stood on the bank of Tuoni's river and raked the waters for her lost Lemminkainen. But she found nothing. She waded stocking-deep into the

172

water. She stood waist-deep among the waves. At last she raked up Lemminkainen's shirt. She raked again, and drew up his stockings. A third time, and she raked up his hat. Full of sorrow, she waded further and raked deeper, and drew up here a finger and there the toes of his left foot, until, piece by piece, she had raked up all that was left of Lemminkainen.

"How shall I make a man again of these pieces?" wept his old mother. "How shall I create the hero anew?"

"You cannot make a man out of these pieces," croaked a raven perched on a bush nearby. "Cast them back into Tuoni's river: perhaps they can be fashioned into a codfish or maybe even a whale."

But the old mother did not heed the raven. Patiently she gathered the fragments, here a rib and there a hand, here the bits of backbone, and there the head, and fitted them all together, bone by bone, and joint by joint. She knit the veins and bound them, and made the flesh firm, with skill and prayer and magic spells. But when all was finished, Lemminkainen remained speechless and without breath.

Then the old mother called upon the bee, the bird of honey, and sent him to fetch nectar from distant flowers, that she might brew a magic ointment that

173

would bring breath and speech back to Lemminkainen. Once and yet again the bee fared forth to collect honey for the precious salve. Once and yet again the old mother tried to brew the wonderful ointment. But in vain.

At last she bade the bee fly over the moon and under the sun and across the shoulder of the Great Bear to the halls of Ukko the Creator, where nectar was boiled in pots of silver and ointment bubbled in kettles of gold. This the bee must fetch for her son's healing. The bee did as she asked, and brought back the precious ointment that had been breathed upon by Ukko, the Creator himself. The old mother smelt it and tasted it and found it good.

She anointed Lemminkainen with the salve in every part, smoothly and surely, and when all was done she spoke to him and said:

"Rise, my son, from your sleep. Waken from your dreams, and come away from this wicked place."

Lemminkainen woke and rubbed his eyes and lifted his voice.

"I have been sleeping a long time," he said. "I have been having very painful dreams."

"You might have slept longer still," said his mother, "you might have had worse dreams yet, if it had not been for your unhappy mother."

174

The Trials of Lemminkainen

Lemminkainen thanked his mother politely for having restored him to life and speech, and related all that had befallen him. His mother listened to his story and rejoiced that he was alive and well, and even handsomer and stronger than before.

"Is there anything further that you want, my son?" she asked. "Is there anything more that you need now?"

"There is one thing," answered Lemminkainen. "My heart is fixed on the beautiful Maiden of the North Country. But her ugly old mother will not give her to me for a wife until I shoot the swan on Tuoni's river and take it back to her as a bride-offering."

"Leave the poor swans in peace," said Lemminkainen's mother. "Have nothing further to do with Tuoni's river, or with anything that swims in its depths or even floats on its surface. Be grateful to Ukko the Creator, with whose help I have brought you back to the light of day. And now come home with me quietly, and go fishing in the clear streams of your own country."

For once Lemminkainen was ready to listen to his old mother's advice and he went quietly home with her. He gave up all thought of wooing the daughter of crafty old Louhi. Indeed he might have forgotten her entirely, but for one thing. The time arrived when

175

old Louhi's beautiful daughter was to be married to Ilmarinen the smith. Lemminkainen, you remember, was the one person who was not invited to the wedding, for fear that he would start a quarrel and spoil the feast. And what came of this, you shall hear.

13

THE UNINVITED GUEST

WHEN Lemminkainen got wind of the fact that there was to be a wedding in the North Country, he asked his mother to warm the bath-house so that he might wash, and to bring him his finest shirt and all his best clothes, that he might be fitly dressed for the feast.

"Do not go, my son," said his wise old mother. "They did not invite you to the wedding, and it is plain that they do not want you."

"A good man needs no invitation," replied Lemminkainen. "And a bright sword with a sharp edge is reason enough to go."

In vain his mother tried to restrain him, warning him of all the terrible dangers of the journey, and reminding him of the evils that had ensnared him once before, when he had been cut to pieces in Tuoni's river. Nothing would stop Lemminkainen. He took his bow from the peg on the wall. He ordered his servant to harness the war-horse. And though his mother followed him with warnings and beseechings, he stepped into his sledge, struck his horse with his beaded whip, and rushed away.

He had not gone far when he came upon a flock of grouse that flew up before his speeding horse. Some of their fallen feathers lay scattered on the ice. Lemminkainen picked these up and put them in his pocket, for one never knows how such things may come in handy.

He drove a little further and suddenly his horse pricked up its ears and neighed in terror. Lemminkainen looked about and saw, even as his mother had warned him, bright danger in his path. There ran a fiery river, and in the river lay a fiery island and on the island stood a flaming mountain and upon its peak perched a fiery eagle. Lemminkainen politely asked the eagle to turn aside and let him pass. But the eagle answered:

"You may pass here and go on to the wedding-feast, but only by traveling into my beak and down my gullet!"

At this Lemminkainen put his hand in his pocket and drew out the grouse-feathers and rubbed them between his palms. Then he breathed on them gently,

178

"There stood a fierce wolf and a huge bear."

and forth from between his fingers flew a flock of grouse. He drove them into the eagle's beak and down his greedy throat. The eagle flew off, satisfied, the fires died down, and so Lemminkainen was free to go on his way.

He had not traveled much further when his horse again showed signs of fright. Lemminkainen looked ahead and saw, even as his mother had warned him, savage danger in his path. There stood a fierce wolf and a huge bear. Quickly he thrust his hand into his pocket, and exploring it, came upon a tuft of ewe's wool that he carried about with him. For one never knows how such things may come in handy. He rubbed the wool between his palms until it was very soft and he breathed on it gently, and forth from between his fingers issued a flock of sheep. The wolf and the bear rushed to devour the sheep, and Lemminkainen passed on safely.

But this was not the last of his troubles. He had to sing a wall of fire into a frozen lake. He had to cast magic spells upon a dreadful viper that crept below a fence made of spears and wattled with serpents, before he came at long last to the cold and misty regions of the North Country. But all the dangers of which his mother had warned him he passed safely, and

181

finally he stood, an uninvited guest, on the threshold of old Louhi's house.

He walked unbidden into the middle of the room and demanded barley for his horse and beer for himself.

The Master of the North Country, angered by his rudeness, bade him lead his horse to the corner where three large hoes rested against the wall and two kettles were standing.

"This is no way to treat the horse of a hero!" cried Lemminkainen. "He will get all sooty from those kettles. In my father's house there was always a clean place for a stranger's horse in the stable, and pegs for a hero to hang his mittens on, and a wall for him to set his sword at rest. I seem to be unwelcome here. You do not even offer me any ale."

"You do not come as a guest," replied crafty old Louhi, the Mistress of the North Country. "You come to humble me. Our ale is still barley, our wheaten bread is not yet baked, and our meat has not been stewed. You should have come last night, or perhaps you should have come tomorrow."

Lemminkainen frowned.

"The feast has been eaten already," said he. "The ale has been drunk, and the pint-pots put away. This was no proper way to hold a wedding-feast. Six times

182

you sent out invitations. Nine times you summoned the lame and the blind and the crippled, the laborer with only one shirt to his back, the scoundrels and the wasters. Everybody was invited. Only me you passed over. And now I am here, a distinguished guest, you do not even offer the hero a mug of beer or a pound of pork."

At that old Louhi bade the little servant-maid give Lemminkainen food and drink. But it was plain that the mistress did not welcome the stranger, so the little maid put meat-bones and fish-heads and old turnip-stalks and dry bread in a dish, and brought a mean pint of ale, and set these before Lemminkainen.

"If you are indeed a hero," said crafty old Louhi, "you can drink this ale without upsetting the can that holds it."

Lemminkainen looked into the ale-can and saw a viper crawling at the bottom and lizards gliding about the rim. He was not disturbed. He put his hand in his pocket and drew out some iron hooks that he had stowed there, not knowing how they might come in handy. He angled in the ale-can with the iron hooks and drew out a hundred toads and a thousand snakes. He threw them on the floor and broke their necks, and then he drank off the ale with gusto. But he was very angry.

183

"I am not honored as a guest," he said. "You should have given me better ale and in a larger vessel. You slaughtered no sheep against my coming, you did not even kill a steer for my meat."

"Why did you come uninvited?" demanded the master of the house.

"A hero needs no invitation," said Lemminkainen impudently. "Give me drink and I will pay you well for it."

Lemminkainen's proud words enraged the Master of the North Country. He sang a pond in front of the stranger, and bade him splash about in that and so satisfy his thirst.

But Lemminkainen answered that he was no calf, to drink river-water. And he sang a mighty ox with golden horns beside the pond to swallow it. Then the Master of the North Country sang a wolf into being to devour the ox. Lemminkainen was not at all disturbed. He sang a white hare onto the floor. But the master of the house sang a dog to devour the hare. Then Lemminkainen sang a squirrel to frolic among the rafters, and the master of the house sang a golden-breasted marten to seize the squirrel. Now it was Lemminkainen's turn to work magic, so he sang a red fox to kill the golden-breasted marten. And when the master of the house sang a hen into being, Lemmin-

184

kainen by his spells created a hawk to tear the hen to pieces.

Now the Master of the North Country was quite out of patience. He ordered Lemminkainen out of the house to which he had come thus boldly uninvited and told him to go home to his own country.

But Lemminkainen refused to leave.

At this the Master of the North Country seized his sword from the wall and declared that they must match weapons, for no other course was open. The lively Lemminkainen was willing enough to fight.

"Let us go out into the field," said the Master of the North Country. "It is awkward fighting in the house: it makes extra work for the women. Blood looks better when it is spilled on the grass. It is very pretty on the snow."

So they went outside. The duel did not last long. Lemminkainen was younger and stronger and quicker than the Master of the North Country. He struck off the old man's head as a turnip is severed from its stalk.

Then old Louhi was filled with rage. She called up a hundred swordsmen and a thousand spearsmen against Lemminkainen. But now that he had avenged the insult of being omitted from the wedding-guests, he was ready enough to go. And he went quickly home to his mother.

185

When his old mother heard all that had happened, she was filled with fear for her son. She knew that crafty old Louhi would not rest till her warriors had slain Lemminkainen. So, giving him a bag of provisions, his mother sent him away to a distant island to hide there from his pursuers.

Lemminkainen reached the far-off island safely. It was a pleasant place, and he made it even pleasanter, singing handsome houses onto its heaths, and pint-pots brimming with ale onto its tables. All the girls of the island rejoiced at his songs and his winning ways. So a year and another year and a third year passed in eating and drinking and dancing and making merry. But at last Lemminkainen was troubled with homesickness. He built himself a boat and sailed home to his own country.

It was no easy journey, and when he finally came to the shores of his own country, horror seized him. Everything was changed from what it had been when he left it. The houses were burned to the ground. The corn-fields had been laid waste. A forest had grown up where his homestead had once stood. There was no sign of a living soul. Lemminkainen wandered about weeping. He knew that the warriors of old Louhi had indeed come and ravaged and spoiled his homeland.

186

The Uninvited Guest

And chiefly he wept for his old mother whom he would never see again.

One day, wandering in the midst of the forest, he came upon a tiny cottage. There, to his wonder and delight, he found his poor old mother again. She was living all alone, waiting patiently for her son's return. She told him the story of how old Louhi's warriors had raged through the country, seeking Lemminkainen and laying the land waste. She told him how they had burned his homestead to ashes. The pair of them wept over the ruins.

But Lemminkainen did not weep long. He was bound to fare forth again to the North Country and give battle to old Louhi's warriors. In vain his mother warned him of all the misfortunes he might meet and reminded him of all the evils he had already endured. Lemminkainen would not listen.

"Besides, mother," he said, "I shall not attempt this alone. I shall get help from my good friend Tiera, that mighty swordsman who was the companion of my boyhood, and together we shall sail against the folk of the North Country. In the old days we fought well side by side. We shall fight even better now."

So Lemminkainen set out to summon his friend Tiera, that together they might take arms against the

187

warriors of the cold and misty regions of the North Country.

When Lemminkainen came to Tiera's homestead he found his friend's mother at the door churning butter and his father at the window carving a spear-shaft. Tiera's brothers were busy making the frame of a sledge and his sisters stood at the bridge-end wringing out the clothes.

Lemminkainen told them why he had come. Tiera's mother stopped churning and his father laid aside his carving and his brothers left the sledge-frame and his sisters put aside the washing, and they all spoke at once, saying that Tiera could not go into battle. He had just taken a young wife and he had promised to stay at home and live in peace with his neighbors.

Tiera himself was sitting by the stove with his feet up, resting. When he heard Lemminkainen's story, he put his feet down and rose from the bench and tightened his belt. He took his sword from the wall and brandished it, and for all that his father and mother and sisters and brothers could say, and in spite of the pleas of his young wife, he followed Lemminkainen down to the ship.

The pair had not sailed far when the news of their venture came to the ears of crafty old Louhi. At once

188

she summoned the Frost and bade him freeze the waters of the lake that borders on the cold and misty regions of the North Country. The Frost wandered over the land, biting the leaves off the trees and the grass in the meadows. He clothed the mountains in ice, and then he came to the lake where Lemminkainen was sailing with his friend. He turned the waters to ice so that the ship stuck fast. He seized on Lemminkainen's fingers. He bit Lemminkainen's toes. But Lemminkainen's lips were free to speak.

"There are plenty of other things for you to freeze," he said to the Frost. "You do not have to attack my fingers and my little toes. Go freeze the willows near the water and the blossoms on the heather and the dough the women are kneading and the milk in the pail. But leave my toes and fingers alone. Otherwise I will send you to the furnace of Hiisi, the Evil One: he will pound you helpless with his hammer."

"Let us understand each other," said the Frost. "I will promise not to injure you any more, if only you won't send me to Hiisi's terrible furnace."

This was well enough, and Lemminkainen's fingers and toes were safe, but still he could not free his boat from the ice. He and his friend Tiera had to walk across the frozen lake, hungry and cold, for a day and another day and a third day. On the third day they

189

came to a wretched village with a castle standing on a hill. There they stopped to ask for meat and fish that the heroes might be fed. But there was neither meat nor fish in that miserable castle, and they had to push on as best they might.

For weeks and months they wandered, suffering and sore, full of laments for the good old days, and wondering if they would ever reach home again. At last Lemminkainen said:

"This trouble is so black that it should at least make us a pair of black horses. Of our evil days my magic can make reins for them, and from my secret sorrows I shall create saddles."

Eagerly Lemminkainen set himself to these tasks, and when he had sung horses and reins and saddles for himself and his companion, they made their sad way home.

There on his little island Lemminkainen had lived ever since, spending most of his time fishing, and thinking mournfully of his many trials, and of how he had been worsted by crafty old Louhi.

All this he told to Vainamoinen and his companions on the red ship.

"It is a dull life I lead here," he said sadly, when his long tale was finished. "It is poor grain that grows on these acres and little fish that comes to my net. You

190

say that you are bound for the dark and misty regions of the North Country, where they eat men and it is said they even drown heroes. I am a tough fellow. I have endured many trials. Take me with you in your red ship."

"We are going to the North Country to capture the magic Sampo," said old Vainamoinen.

"It was I who fashioned it," said Ilmarinen the smith. "But little good I got of it. I did not even get a wife for my trouble."

"Take me with you," begged Lemminkainen. "I have long held a grudge against that crafty old witch, the Mistress of the North Country. I will help you win the Sampo away from her."

"Climb in," said old Vainamoinen. "Another hero will not sink the ship. You may give us good help in combat."

Joyfully Lemminkainen boarded the red ship. Swiftly they hoisted sail, and the vessel moved like a bird across the waves.

They sailed for a whole day and for another day through the waters of the marshes and on the third day they reached a furious waterfall. It needed all Vainamoinen's spells to pass it safely. But he steered the red ship among the sharp rocks and through the raging foam and out again into the open sea.

191

But no sooner had they escaped the waterfall than suddenly the vessel halted and stood grounded. But how and on what, nobody knew.

And what obstructed their passage, and what befel them on their further journey, you shall hear.

14

THE CAPTURE OF THE SAMPO

SEEING that the ship was stuck fast, old Vaina-moinen bade the newcomer stoop down and see what was wrong.

"Look and see whether the ship has grounded on the rocks there below, or whether it is caught among floating branches."

Lemminkainen leaned over and peered into the depths.

"The ship is not resting on the rocks," said he. "It is not caught in floating branches. It is grounded on the broad shoulders of a pike, on the backbone of a water-dog."

"Plunge your sword into the water," commanded Vainamoinen, "and cut the fish in half."

Lemminkainen drew his good blade and plunged it into the water, but instead of striking the fish with it, he fell overboard. He might have drowned, but the

193

smith Ilmarinen seized him by the hair and pulled him back into the boat.

"You pretend you are a man," he said, as he dragged the dripping Lemminkainen to safety. "You think you are a bearded hero. But you are only a helpless boy."

Then Ilmarinen the smith drew his own sword and struck the great pike a furious blow. But the blade shivered to pieces and the fish was not even scratched.

"You are not even half a man," said old Vainamoinen scornfully. "You are not the third part of a hero. For this task we need skill and strength and knowledge."

Then lusty old Vainamoinen drew his sword and thrust it into the water under the boat at the great shoulders and strong backbone of the pike. But the sword stuck fast in the pike's terrible jaws. This did not trouble Vainamoinen. He lifted his sword and heaved up the great pike on the point of it, and dragged the fish out of the water and sliced it in two. The tail fell back into the water and the head he hoisted on deck.

Now the prow of the ship was free and the vessel moved on smoothly. Vainamoinen stood at the rudder and guided it to the shore.

"This is a fine pike's head," he said. "Let the

194

strongest men among you carve it up, and the girls can cook it for our dinner."

"The hero who caught the fish can carve it best," they answered.

So Vainamoinen took his sharp sword and cut the huge fish-head into pieces. The girls minced the flesh and cooked it and they had a fine fish dinner. As for the bones, they were scattered on the rocks.

But wise old Vainamoinen looked at the bones and wondered if they too could not be put to some use. He turned to his brother the smith.

"Suppose you took these jaw-bones to the smithy," he said. "You ought to be able to make something of them, and those great teeth too."

"The most skilful smith in the world could forge nothing of fish-bones," answered Ilmarinen.

"Nevertheless," said Vainamoinen, "there is stuff there for a harp, if we had a clever workman."

In the whole ship there was no clever workman. But old Vainamoinen was not daunted. He set to work himself, and constructed a harp, the kind that is called a kantele. He used the pike's jaw-bones for the frame, and the pike's teeth for pegs, and horsehair for the strings. It was a wonderful kantele.

The young men and the grown heroes, and the

195

half-grown boys and the little girls, and the maidens and the married women, all gathered about admiring the work of his hands. One after another they tried to play on Vainamoinen's kantele, but they could draw no music from it.

"How stupid you all are!" cried Ilmarinen. "That is not the way to play on a harp of fish-bone. Let me try." But though he turned it this way and that, he could not make a tune.

Then Lemminkainen took up the kantele, but he fared no better. No matter how he tried to play on it, the strings tangled, the horsehair whined, and the sound was so harsh that everybody had a headache. Finally one old man grumbled that he had been kept awake for a week with the ugly noise and he told them to throw the kantele back into the water.

"No," said the kantele. "I will not be thrown into the water. Let him who made me play upon me, and then you shall hear me sing."

So they carried the kantele to Vainamoinen. He washed his hands, and then he sat down on the singer's stone, the stone of joy, and propped the harp on his knee and stretched his fingers and lifted his thumbs and began to play.

One pleasure followed another as he turned the pegs made of the pike's teeth and plucked at the horsehair

196

strings. Sweetly and clearly the music sounded. The squirrels climbed on the nearest branches to hear. The wolves wakened in their lairs. The bears came loping and sat on the fences to listen. The fences broke, and the bears climbed into the pine-trees, and the pine-trees listened too. The birds of the air assembled to hear the music, the eagle and the hawk, the ducks and the swans from the snowy marshes. The small birds came flying and perched on Vainamoinen's shoulders. Shoals of fishes came swimming shoreward to hear the wonderful kantele. The Cloud-Maidens dropped their golden shuttles and leaned from the rainbow to listen. The water-nymphs left off combing their hair with their silver combs, and floated up to hear him, with their hair all tangled. The Mother of Waters rose from the waves and climbed on a rock to listen to Vainamoinen's playing.

He played for a day and a second day and a third day, and the strong men and the married women, the girls and the half-grown boys and the little children all marveled at the music. It was so beautiful that they wept with joy. Even wise Vainamoinen, hearing the sweet strains that came from the kantele, fell to weeping himself, so keen was his delight. His tears were larger than cranberries, much larger than peas, rounder than the eggs of the grouse. They rolled down his

197

cheeks and over his chin, till five woollen cloaks were damp and six golden girdles were wet with them, and ten overcoats were all soaking. The tears rolled down and made a salt pool and flowed away and fell into the lake.

"Is there anyone here," asked old Vainamoinen, "who can gather the tears I have shed? I will give a cloak of fine feathers to whoever gathers my tears and brings them back to me."

The duck was eager for a new feather cloak, and besides, she was used to plunging into the water. So she went in search of Vainamoinen's tears. She found them, too, at the very bottom of the lake, but when she brought them back to the famous singer, the tears had turned into beautiful blue pearls, fit for a king's mantle. All this happened because of the music of the wonderful kantele.

But now Vainamoinen said they must tarry no longer. Music was a fine thing, but they must not forget that they had set out to fetch the magic Sampo, the work of the smith Ilmarinen.

So once more the company boarded the red ship, with Ilmarinen at the head of the rowers, and Lemminkainen in the stern, and old Vainamoinen at the rudder.

For long and long the red ship sailed onward, and

at last it came within sight of the cold and misty regions of the North Country.

Swiftly the vessel was pulled to shore and the company disembarked. Swiftly they marched to the house of the dread Mistress of the North Country and crowded into the hall.

Old Louhi greeted the heroes and asked them why they had come.

"We have come because of the magic Sampo," answered lusty old Vainamoinen. "Everywhere men speak of this marvellous treasure. We too want to behold its many-colored lid. We too want to share in the bounty it provides."

"Two men cannot share a small grouse," said the crafty old Mistress of the North Country. "Three men cannot divide a rabbit among them. I am the Mistress of the Sampo, and here it will remain, with me and my people."

"If you will not share the bounty of the magic Sampo with us," said old Vainamoinen, "then give us half of it to carry home with us to the Land of Heroes. Half of a magic mill like that will be sufficient."

At this old Louhi grew very angry. She was not going to give up any part of the magic mill. Let them take it by force if they could. And she summoned the warriors of the North Country, the young men and the

199

strong men, bidding them lift their swords against these daring beggars, and first of all slice off the head of old Vainamoinen.

But the oldest magician sat down quietly and set his kantele on his knee and commenced to play. So sweet and merry was the tune he played that all who heard it were filled with delight. The women began to laugh, the men wept with joy, and finally young and old, all the folk of the North Country, hearing the soft strains of this music, fell into a deep sleep. Even crafty old Louhi sank into slumber.

Then old Vainamoinen went to the hill of copper within whose heart the magic Sampo was hidden, fastened with nine strong locks and secured by ten strong bolts. There he stood and sang until the doors of the mountain shook and the iron hinges trembled. Thereupon Ilmarinen took butter and bacon-fat and rubbed the hinges with it so that they would not creak, and with his strong fingers the smith lifted the bars and bolts and broke the locks to bits and threw open the heavy doors. There stood the magic Sampo with its lid of many colors, turning and grinding out wealth of corn and salt and coins.

"Go and seize the lid of the Sampo," said the oldest magician to young Lemminkainen.

Eagerly he ran forward, boasting of his strength,

but though he pushed with his arms and his chest and his knees, he could not move the Sampo from its three strong roots or budge the many-colored lid.

Now there was a huge bull in the meadow, with horns a fathom long and a mighty muzzle and sinews of enormous strength. He was fetched from the field and set to tugging at the magic mill. It was not long before he pulled up the roots of the Sampo. The magic mill began to move, and the many-colored lid was loosened. Lusty old Vainamoinen and his brother the smith and lively young Lemminkainen all pulled and tugged together. They lifted the mighty Sampo and carried it out of the hill of copper and bore it off to their ship. They stowed the magic mill in the hold and pushed off into the water.

Vainamoinen called upon the wind to work with the rowers and blow the ship away from the dark and misty shores of the North Country, and he asked the help of the Master of Waters, so that they might sail home swiftly. He stood at the rudder, and the smith and young Lemminkainen pulled at the oars, and they sailed for a day and another day and a third day without stopping.

Again and again the rowers asked old Vainamoinen to cheer them with a song, but he always replied that it was too soon to rejoice. There would be time enough

201

for singing when they had brought the magic Sampo safely to the Land of Heroes.

"We must have a song now," asserted Lemminkainen. "If you will not give us one, then I will do the singing myself. My voice may not be very sweet, but it is good and loud."

And he commenced to sing. Indeed his voice was not sweet, but hoarse and harsh, and so noisy that the sound traveled across the water until it was heard in six villages. Now in a swamp nearby a crane was standing on a stump preparing to count the bones in his toes. He had just lifted up one foot when he heard the voice of Lemminkainen. He was so terrified by the sound that he flew from his perch screaming, and he did not stop flying, shrieking as he flew, until he came to that part of the North Country where the host of people was lying wrapped in slumber.

Old Louhi, the Mistress of the North Country, was the first to be awakened by his screams. She hurried out into the farmyard to see if her cattle had been stolen or if her corn had been plundered. All was in order. Then she went to the hill of copper. The locks were broken, the iron hinges cracked, the doors stood open. She looked in, and saw that the Sampo had been taken away.

Filled with grief and rage, the old woman called
202

upon the Cloud-Maiden to send a thick fog over the water so that old Vainamoinen could not see to steer his ship. Then she summoned the sea-monster, Iku-Turso, to raise his dreadful head out of the deep and drown those who had seized the Sampo. Finally she called upon Ukko, the Creator himself, to raise a mighty tempest and destroy Vainamoinen with wind and wave.

"But do not sink the ship!" she cried. "Let the Sampo come floating back safely to its home in the North Country!"

The Cloud-Maiden obeyed old Louhi's behest and sent a thick fog over the water. For three days old Vainamoinen did not turn his rudder, not knowing which way to steer. But on the third day he declared:

"It is a weak man who lets himself be worsted by mist. Not the laziest of heroes would submit to a fog."

So saying, he dipped his sword into the waves and when he withdrew it, the blade was dripping not sea-water but honey. At that the fog lifted from the sea, and the ship was able to sail on.

But they had not gone far when they heard a terrific roar rising out of the water. The waves lashed at the red ship and the foam flew wildly. Even Ilmarinen the smith was frightened. His face grew pale. He pulled his cap over his ears and covered his eyes with

203

his hands. But lusty old Vainamoinen looked over the side of the ship to see what was causing the commotion. It was no trifle that he saw.

It was the sea-monster, Iku-Turso, whom old Louhi had called to destroy them. This did not daunt the oldest magician. He grasped Iku-Turso by the ears and dragged him up out of the water and asked him what he was doing there. Iku-Turso did not like this reception. But he was not disturbed by it either. He did not answer. Three times Vainamoinen asked him why he had come. Only at the third question Iku-Turso replied.

"I came at the bidding of the witch, old Louhi of the North Country," he gasped. "But if you spare my life, I promise you I will not lift my head again in the sight of men."

At that old Vainamoinen flung the sea-monster back into the deep.

"See that you keep your promise!" he said sternly.

And from that time to this the sea-monster has never raised his head from the billows into the light of day or by night either.

So the ship sailed onward, but they had not journeyed far when, at the bidding of old Louhi, Ukko the Creator raised a terrible tempest. The winds rose in fury. The west wind blew fiercely, the south-west

"He grasped Iku-Turso by the ears and dragged him up out of the water."

wind blew just as fiercely, the south wind blew even more fiercely. The east wind whistled, the south-east wind roared, and the north wind howled. The trees on shore lost all their leaves, the needles of the pines were swept away, the heather lost its flowerets, the grasses their tassels, and the black ooze in the depths of the sea was stirred to froth and heaved up to the surface of the water. The winds blew so wildly that they seized the pike-bone harp, Vainamoinen's precious kantele, and carried it off to the kingdom of the sea.

Vainamoinen cried out in grief at the loss of his kantele. But Ilmarinen the smith groaned with fear.

"Sailors do not groan!" shouted old Vainamoinen then. "A ship is no place for tears!" And he began to speak gently to the waves, and begged the winds to go quietly home to their families. The waves listened to the oldest magician. And the winds went home to their relations.

But the ship had been badly injured by the storm. It took all their strength and skill to repair the damage. Finally all was in order, and they could sail onward.

Meanwhile old Louhi, the crafty Mistress of the North Country, seeing that her work had been in vain, determined on a new course. And what it was, and how the heroes fared, you shall hear.

15

THE DESTRUCTION OF
THE SAMPO

OLD Louhi's first act was to summon all the
warriors of the North Country. She armed
them with bows and arrows and sharp swords, and then
she fitted out a mighty war-ship. There were a hundred swordsmen on board and a thousand men with
cross-bows in the tall ship. Old Louhi herself lifted
the mast, and spread the canvas. The main-sail was so
wide that it hung like a cloud in heaven. Thus they
set forth to give battle to old Vainamoinen and recap-
ture the magic Sampo.

Now lusty old Vainamoinen had already overcome
many dangers, but he felt in his bones that he must be
wary, and ever keep on guard against greater trouble.
So he sent young Lemminkainen to the look-out to see
what he could see.

Lemminkainen climbed up the masthead of the

red ship, among the bellowing sails, and looked east and west and northwest and south and over toward the dark and misty shores of the North Country.

"The horizon is clear before us," he called down, "but behind us in the north there is a cloud, a small cloud, off to the northwest."

"Nonsense," said old Vainamoinen. "There can be no cloud there. Look again."

Lemminkainen looked again more sharply.

"I see an island in the distance," he called down. "A far-away island, covered with trees. There are falcons and speckled grouse perched on the branches."

"Nonsense!" exclaimed old Vainamoinen. "There can be no falcons there and no speckled grouse. Look again."

So Lemminkainen looked over the waters a third time.

"I see a ship!" he shouted, "a ship sailing from the North Country. There are a hundred men at the oars and a thousand bowmen beside them."

"Row, brother smith!" cried Vainamoinen. "Row, Ilmarinen, as fast as you can! And you, Lemminkainen, climb down and pull at the oars. All of you, row as hard and as fast as you can!"

At once everybody in the red ship set to work and rowed mightily, straining at the pinewood oars. The

209

prow dashed forward like a seal in flight, the waves boiled and the foam flew. The heroes pulled at the oars as if they were rowing for a wager. They strove as though they were racing. But though they used all their strength, they did not widen the distance between them and the war-ship from the North Country.

Now they were indeed in serious trouble. Misfortune was on their tracks. Old Vainamoinen thought that doomsday was falling on his head. But he was not one to be daunted. He considered what it was best to do. It was not long before the oldest magician thought of a plan whereby he could outwit the Mistress of the North Country.

He took a small piece of tinder from his tinder-box and threw it over his left shoulder, and as it flew through the air he uttered a spell. Thanks to Vainamoinen's magic, the tinder no sooner struck the water than it grew up into a sharp cliff that jutted east and north. Old Louhi's ship, rushing forward at tremendous speed, dashed against this cliff, wedged against the rocks, and splintered. The masts crashed into the water, the sails were carried away by the wind. Vainly old Louhi tried to raise her ship. The ribs were staved in, the oar-locks were shattered.

But crafty old Louhi was not without magic of her own. She took five sharp scythes and six worn-out hoes

210

and fashioned them into talons. Then she seized the broken planks of her ship and turned them into wings, and of the rudder she fashioned a tail. And the scythes and the hoes and the planks and the rudder became a mighty eagle. When all was finished, old Louhi herself took the shape of the eagle she had contrived. And under her wings she took a hundred of her swordsmen, and on her tail she carried a thousand archers.

Then she flew, flapping one wing against the clouds and trailing one wing in the water, to attack old Vainamoinen. She swept over the sea and perched on the masthead of his red ship. The boat lurched sideways with the weight of the eagle, and of the fighters clinging to its wings and riding on its tail. Old Vainamoinen thought that his red ship would surely sink under the load.

He looked up at the masthead and hailed the terrible bird.

"I know that you want the Sampo," he said. "And so do we heroes of the Land of Heroes. But the magic mill is big enough for all of us. Let us carry it to shore and divide it, half for the folk of the North Country and half for us of the Land of Heroes. Even a piece of the magic Sampo will work well enough to give us great plenty."

"Never will I share the Sampo!" cried old Louhi

211

fiercely. And without further talk she swooped down to seize the magic mill by force.

Young Lemminkainen whipped out his sword and struck at the eagle, but to no purpose. Then old Vainamoinen lifted the rudder and smote with all his might. A hundred swordsmen dropped from the eagle's wings, a thousand archers tumbled from her tail. There was savage fighting on the red ship, and the warriors of the North Country were overwhelmed and drowned in the sea. Old Vainamoinen struck and struck again. At last the eagle dropped upon the deck. Vainamoinen's blows had broken every claw but one. Only the tiniest remained.

But old Louhi was firm in her purpose. With the single small claw that was left her she dragged at the Sampo by its many-colored lid and pulled it out of the ship's hold, and cast it into the water. But small good this did her, for the magic Sampo broke into fragments and the many-colored lid was smashed to splinters. The larger pieces were so heavy that they sank beneath the waves, where they have lain ever since, producing the wealth of the sea. The smaller pieces floated on the surface of the waters, rocked by the waves and wafted hither and yon by the winds.

Old Vainamoinen watched them tossing about and he rejoiced at the sight, for he could gather the fragments that floated to shore and bear them off to the Land of Heroes to create riches for all the folk of that country.

"Aha, old Louhi!" he cried. "You have done well for us. You have done very well. Even the pieces of the Sampo are good magic. Our ploughing and our sowing will prosper! Our crops will grow in the sunlight and shine like silver in the pleasant moonlight. Our cattle will feed in the sun and in the pleasant moonlight they shall have increase."

But the eagle that was crafty old Louhi screamed vengefully:

"You may have the better part of the Sampo, but your crops will not prosper nor your cattle increase. I shall find ways to prevent it, if I must steal the lights out of the sky."

Then with her one remaining claw she seized a tiny piece of the Sampo's many-colored lid and carried it back with her to the North Country, lamenting her loss as she flew. For this poor fragment of the magic mill could bring small blessings to those cold and misty regions, and it would be a starved life that her folk would lead there without the Sampo. So, shrieking and wailing, she flew homeward.

But lusty old Vainamoinen paid little heed to old Louhi's threats. He too went back to his own coun-

213

try, carrying with him in his red ship many pieces of the magic Sampo that he had picked up from the shore. When he reached home, he planted them in the earth, that they might grow and flourish and the land be rich in barley and the flowing ale that is brewed of the barley-grain, and rich in rye and the crusty bread that is made of the rye-flour.

The capture of so many pieces of the Sampo and the thought of the harvest filled old Vainamoinen with joy.

"Now is the time for music and pleasure. Now is the time for singing," he said. But then he sighed, for the kantele that he had wrought of the pike's head was sunk to the bottom of the sea.

Yet he would not despair. He summoned his brother the smith.

"Go to your smithy, Ilmarinen," he said, "and forge me a rake of iron. Set the teeth close together and make the handle five hundred fathoms long. I must rake among the reeds of the lake and in the rocky caverns of the salmon and among the crooked paths of the fishes under the sea. I am going to rake the waves for my lost kantele."

Ilmarinen was glad to be of service. He too wanted to hear again the lovely strains of the kantele. So he forged a rake with a copper handle. The teeth were a

214

hundred fathoms in length and the copper handle full five hundred fathoms.

Vainamoinen took the rake and went down to the shore and stepped into a boat to sail in search of his lost treasure. He sailed here and there. He raked among the shore-drift and the leaves of the water-lilies. He raked the shoals and the deeps as well, but his harp of pike-bone he did not find. Sadly he returned home, with his head bowed and his cap awry. He left his boat on the beach and his rake beside it, and he wandered on the edge of the woodland, wishing for his lost kantele.

He had not gone far when he heard a sound of weeping. It came from a speckled birch. Old Vainamoinen hurried to where the birch-tree was standing. He was in a mood to sympathize with whatever mourned.

"What are you crying about?" he asked.

"Oh," wailed the birch-tree, "I have cause enough to cry. There is no tree in the forest that is so cruelly used as I am. In the spring the children come with their sharp knives and cut me and carve me. In summer the wicked herdsmen strip my bark away to plait themselves berry-baskets. Girls come to dance beneath my branches and pull off my crown for their whisk-brooms. The young men cut off my boughs to get faggots for burning. And in winter I shiver and shake, leafless and scarred and stripped, in the snow and the wind. There is no tree so hacked and hewed as I."

"Do not cry, little birch-tree," said old Vainamoinen gently. "There is happiness in store for you. I will make you sing for pleasure."

Indeed he spoke truly. For of the tough birch-wood old Vainamoinen fashioned the frame of a new kantele. It was firm and fine and its curves were curves of beauty. Now he needed pegs for his harp. There was a splendid oak standing in the farm-yard. On every branch hung an acorn and on every acorn perched a cuckoo, and every cuckoo was sounding five clear notes, and as the notes sounded, silver and gold fell from their beaks upon the ground. Old Vainamoinen gathered the silver and gold for the pegs of his new kantele. But still he had no harp-strings. Without five harp-strings, the beautiful birch-wood frame and the gold and silver pegs would never make music.

Lusty old Vainamoinen went wandering along the heath thinking where he could find them. Now there was a young girl sitting on the heath, singing softly to herself while she waited for her sweetheart to come and meet her. Old Vainamoinen heard her singing and

216

he went up to her and spoke to her gently and begged her politely to give him a few strands of her hair. The girl was willing, and gave him five strands of her strong lovely hair, and of these he wrought his harp-strings.

Then old Vainamoinen sat down on a rock and propped the knob of his new kantele on his knee and turned the frame toward heaven, and adjusted the strings. And then with all his fingers he drew forth the most delicious music. The birch-wood rang out joyfully, the pegs given by the golden cuckoos turned smoothly, and the hair of the young girl waiting for her sweetheart sang like a happy heart.

At the sound of Vainamoinen's new kantele the mountains trembled and the plains shook, the gravel stirred in the water, the pine-trees rejoiced on the hill and even the old stumps on the heath began to skip for pleasure. All the folk of the Land of Heroes came running to hear the music. Laughing girls and smiling mothers, men holding their caps in their fists, and old women with their hands at their sides, all trooped toward Vainamoinen, exclaiming over the wonderful kantele. The beasts of the forest rested on their paws to hear the melody, the birds perched on the branches near the harper, the fish swam to the surface of the sea to listen, and even the worms turned around in the earth and crept to the top of the soil to hear Vaina-moinen's music.

He played for a whole day and for another day and for a third day, every morning right after breakfast. And he did not stop to put on a fresh girdle and he wore the same shirt for three days, because he did not want to pause in his playing to change it. Part of the time he played walking through the pine-wood, and then every needle on the pines rejoiced to hear him. And part of the time he sat in his own house playing, and then the roof rang and the boards resounded and the ceilings sang and the doors creaked happily and the windows laughed, and even the stones of the hearth were stirred by the enchanting music of Vaina-moinen's birch-wood kantele.

But while he had been fashioning his new harp and delighting all the folk of the Land of Heroes with his singing, old Louhi, the crafty Mistress of the North Country, had been brooding over the loss of the magic Sampo. When finally the news reached her of how Vainamoinen had gathered the broken pieces of the Sampo and planted them in the Land of Heroes, and of how they had flourished there, old Louhi was filled with jealousy. And when she heard that Vainamoinen was traveling about playing the harp and singing songs

220

about the prosperity of his country, then old Louhi was very angry indeed.

She called upon Ukko the Creator to send an iron hail or a deadly plague upon the folk of the Land of Heroes.

"Let the men die in the farm-yard and the women die on the floor of the cow-shed. Let the whole people perish!" cried old Louhi in her rage.

But she knew well enough that if her curse was to be effective, she herself must work her evil magic. And how she did this and what came of it, you shall hear.

16

THE LAST ADVENTURE

NOW it happened that the blackest and ugliest of the daughters of Tuoni, Lord of the Dead, had wandered to the North Country and there given birth to nine hideous children. And in the time of childbirth it was crafty old Louhi, the Mistress of the North Country, who had helped her and cared for her. The names of four of these children were Colic and Itch and Gout and Plague, and there were four more as ugly, but the ninth and the nastiest was Envy. It was these horrid creatures that old Louhi sent forth to the Land of Heroes to destroy its people.

Great then was the misery in that country. The singing was changed to wailing and the laughter to tears. Lusty old Vainamoinen put aside his kantele and with fire and water he made magic against the dread diseases. Then he took his sharp sword and drove them to the Mount of Torments, where the stones would not weep for pain nor the rocks complain of aching. With eight soothing salves and nine magic drugs old Vainamoinen rubbed and anointed the sick till all were sound and hale. The diseases were sealed up in a barrel and locked fast in the Mount of Torments. And Envy was banished with them.

The folk of the Land of Heroes were full of gratitude to the oldest magician and to Ukko the Creator, who had helped him to dispel all these evils. But the news that her sorcery was in vain was not pleasing to old Louhi, when it came at last to her ears, and she set to work to devise another way of injuring those who possessed the pieces of the magic Sampo. She awakened the great Bear of the heath from his slumbers, and drove him to the Land of Heroes to work ill among its people.

But old Vainamoinen called upon his brother the smith to forge him a new spear with a copper shaft and three cutting edges. Then with Ilmarinen's handiwork he went forth against the shaggy monster.

It was not long before the old huntsman returned victorious. Then great was the rejoicing. The honey-eater was stripped of his skin, and the flesh was cut up and placed in cauldrons of copper and gilded kettles. There it simmered away, till the meat was sweet, and then it was heaped on brimming platters and carried

223

to the tables beside great mugs of red ale. There was enough bear-steak for an abundant feast and more than enough to be salted away. It was evening before the feast was over, and then the time was come for singing. So lusty old Vainamoinen took his kantele and played so sweetly that the moon came from his house and stood on a crooked birch-tree to listen and the sun came from his castle and sat on a fir-tree to hear.

But crafty old Louhi, the Mistress of the North Country, was ill content. Instead of destroying the folk of the Land of Heroes, the honey-eater had provided them with a fat feast. Still, she had not come to the end of her evil magic.

She set to work to capture the sun from the top of the fir-tree and to seize the moon from the birch-tree. She carried the lights of heaven home with her to the dark and misty regions of the North Country, and there she hid them in a mountain as hard as steel among rocks as strong as iron. The Land of Heroes was left in cold and darkness. The sky was filled with night, and the house of Ukko the Creator was as dismal as the lightless homes in Vainamoinen's country.

Ukko the Creator felt strange indeed without his moon or his sun, so he walked out in his blue stockings to the edge of the clouds and the borders of the

224

"She set to work to capture the sun from the top of the fir-tree and to seize the moon from the birch-tree."

heavens to seek them. But he could not find any sign of them. Then he took his sword and struck it against his finger-nail and a bright spark flew forth. Ukko gave the spark to one of the Maidens of the Air to tend, hoping to fashion a new sun of this brightness. But the stupid Maiden of the Air dropped it and it fell flaming through the six spangled vaults of heaven and fell into a lake.

The waters of the lake boiled up. All the fishes rushed to seize the spark that was destroying their watery homes, and in the end it was swallowed by a herring. The unhappy creature swam up and down, tormented by the fiery spark, till a salmon-trout, tired of its complaints, gulped it down. Now it was the salmon-trout's turn to swim up and down in burning misery, until a great grey pike came forward and swallowed the salmon-trout who had swallowed the herring who had swallowed the fiery spark.

Old Vainamoinen had seen the spark fall from the sky and he was eager to get hold of it, for he too hoped it would replace the light of the stolen sun and moon. He went out onto the lake where it had fallen and there the fishes told him the story of what had happened. But try as he might, Vainamoinen could not capture the grey pike.

227

At last he returned home and prepared a linen net of the fairest flax, a net of a hundred meshes. He placed this in his boat, and taking along his brother Ilmarinen, he set forth once more. He cast the linen net into the water and drew it and dragged it, and many a perch and many a salmon-trout and many a bream came to his net, but never the grey pike with the spark of fire in his belly. All Vainamoinen's labors were in vain.

But he had a friend, a dwarf, a very small hero, and the dwarf came down to the shore of the lake and lifted a pine-tree from the bank and threshed the water with it till the fish swam by hundreds into Vainamoinen's net. The oldest magician urged his boat with its heavy load to the red bridge-end, and there he sorted out the fishes. Among them was the grey pike.

But Vainamoinen knew that it was a risky thing to take bare-handed a fish with a spark of fire in its belly. For such a task he needed iron gloves or gauntlets of stone or perhaps copper mittens. While he was reflecting what he had best do, the son of the Sun spoke to him and said:

"Do not fret, old Vainamoinen. I will venture to take the grey pike in my own hands, for fire will not hurt me, and I will rip him up with the knife my

228

father gave me. It has a golden haft and a silver blade."

With these words the son of the Sun dropped down beside old Vainamoinen and took his knife from his belt and ripped open the body of the grey pike. There was the salmon-trout and within it lay the smooth-skinned herring. The son of the Sun split open the herring and found a blue clew in the third fold of its entrails. He unwound it and found a red clew. In the middle of the red clew was the spark of fire itself.

"How shall I carry it to the cold dark dwellings of the Land of Heroes?" Vainamoinen wondered.

But before he could think of a plan the spark flew up and singed the hands of the son of the Sun and singed the beard of lusty old Vainamoinen. His brother the smith was standing beside him. The spark leaped up and singed the hands and scorched the cheeks of Ilmarinen so terribly that he had to run to the shore of the lake and cry to Ukko the Creator for ice and hoar-frost with which to soothe his stinging burns.

But lusty old Vainamoinen was not to be daunted. He thrust the fiery spark into a piece of tinder and carried it to the hearths and kettles of his people to give light and heat for cooking.

Still, it was of no use as a substitute for the stolen

229

sun and moon. The crops were consumed by frost. The cattle suffered. The birds of the air felt strange in this enduring night. And the folk of the Land of Heroes mourned in darkness. They never knew whether it was morning or evening. It was indeed hard to live without the lights of the sky.

They came to Ilmarinen the smith and begged him to forge them a new sun and a new moon out of silver and gold. He labored long at the task, and when the false sun and moon were finished, he lifted them and set them up, the one on the tip of a birch-tree and the other on the summit of a fir. But though they were very beautiful, they did not shine like sunlight and like moonlight.

Then the oldest magician took counsel with himself and made magic with a handful of sticks from the boughs of the alder. He questioned the sticks and they told him that the real sun and moon were hidden deep in the stone mountain in the dark and misty regions of the North Country.

So old Vainamoinen took ship and sailed for that place to demand the lights of heaven.

"You may have them," said old Louhi's warriors mockingly, "if you overcome us in open combat."

Now old Vainamoinen's sword was longer than theirs by only so much as a barley-grain or perhaps the
230

width of a corn-stalk. But he sliced off their heads like turnip-tops and went forthwith to the stone mountain to fetch what he had come for.

There were nine doors and a hundred bolts to the stone mountain. There were dreadful serpents guarding the stolen treasures. It was a trifle for the oldest magician to destroy the serpents. But not all his spells were sufficient to break the bolts and move the heavy doors.

Very much annoyed, he went home, and sought out his brother the smith.

"You must forge me mighty spears and a dozen hatchets," he said. "You must give me a bunch of enormous keys to open the doors of the stone mountain. Otherwise I shall never be able to get at the sun and moon."

Ilmarinen set to work at once. He made a great bundle of spears and he forged twelve strong hatchets and then he began making a bunch of enormous keys. The noise in the smithy was so loud that it thundered far off in the cold and misty regions of the North Country. Old Louhi heard the clatter and the clamor. She was fearful of what it might mean. So she took the form of a hawk and came flying to the Land of Heroes.

She flew straight to Ilmarinen's smithy. She flew

231

so fast that the smith thought a fierce wind was blowing. He went to the window of his smithy to see what he could see. But he found only the grey hawk that was old Louhi.

"What are you doing here outside my window, O bird of prey?" he inquired.

"I have come to watch you at work," answered crafty old Louhi. "You are indeed a marvellous smith. What skilful fingers you have and what mighty arms!" she said, flattering him. "You are truly a wonderful craftsman."

"It is no wonder," answered Ilmarinen. "It was I who forged the heavens and I who welded the arch of the air."

"But what are you making now, O smith?" asked the hawk. "What are you forging this time?"

"I am forging a collar," replied Ilmarinen. "I am making a ring for the neck of the wicked Mistress of the North Country. When this work is done she will be firmly fettered forever to the side of a great mountain."

When old Louhi heard these words she felt her doom coming upon her. Filled with fear she flew swiftly back to her own country. She did not stop until she had come to the place where she had hidden the lights of heaven. Quickly she freed the sun and moon

232

from hiding. Then, taking the shape of a pigeon, she flew back to Ilmarinen's smithy.

"What are you doing here, O pigeon?" asked the smith. "Why are you perched on my threshold?"

"I have come to bring you news," said old Louhi. "The moon has risen out of the stone. The sun is freed from the rock."

Ilmarinen did not wait to see the bird depart for the North Country, nevermore to return. He hurried but of the dark smithy into the open, and gazed anxiously at the sky. There he saw that the moon was truly gleaming on high and the sun was shining as before. At once he rushed to the house of his brother, old Vainamoinen.

"Come, brother!" he cried. "Here is something for a singer to see! The moon is shining and the sun is shining too. They have been restored to their places in the heavens. Come and look!"

Lusty old Vainamoinen hurried out into the open and lifted up his head, and there indeed he saw the moon risen and the sun beaming freely.

"Hail, fair-cheeked Moon!" he cried. "You are a silver dove in the heavens. And you, bright Sun, like a golden cuckoo! How good it is to see you again! Now you may travel on your accustomed ways, and bring us health and increase."

233

Now as never before was a time for singing. Lusty old Vainamoinen took his birch-wood kantele and sang sweetly and surely. He sang of the lights of heaven and of the prospering earth. He sang of the Land of Heroes and its people, their sorrows and their feasts and their great deeds. He sang the story of the magic Sampo. He sang too of his own childhood and of his strange birth in the beginning of the beginning.

For it came to pass that the Virgin of the Air, tiring of her lonely life in the upper regions, descended to the surface of the sea. There she mated with the wind, and became the Mother of Waters, but it was long and long before she bore the child Vainamoinen. And as she swam restlessly back and forth, a teal came flying in search of a dwelling. Then the Mother of Waters lifted up her knee and on her knee the teal made its nest and laid a great egg. The egg was so heavy a burden that the Mother of Waters moved her knee, and the egg fell into the water and broke. But it was not lost. The under half of the shell turned to solid earth, and the upper half to the arch of heaven. The yolk became the sun and the white of the egg was the bright moon. Then the Mother of Waters, swimming amid the waves, pointed with her finger and produced the rocky headlands, and stepped over the depths of the sea and left in her footprints the caves

234

of the fishes. She set all Creation in order. But the child Vainamoinen had not yet been born. Long and long he rested in his mother's body, but it was a narrow room he found there and he longed for freedom. He too wished to see the lights of heaven and the stars of the Great Bear. He begged them to help him come forth. But they could not help him to be born. At last by his own mighty efforts he issued forth and floated on the surface of the sea, admiring the sun and moon and the stars of the Great Bear. Thus was born the oldest magician and the wisest and sweetest of singers.

All this Vainamoinen sang anew, playing the while on his birch-wood kantele with his ten fingers, so that the folk rejoiced to hear him. There was no song too strange and no music too wonderful for him. And the old men listened and nodded, and the young men heard and applauded. The women laughed for pleasure and the young girls were dancing. And all the little children marveled.

But lusty old Vainamoinen could not remain forever in one place. He could not sing always. He felt the need for journeying further. So he boarded his ship, a splendid ship with a copper deck, and he took his birch-wood kantele on his arm, and bade the Land of Heroes farewell.

None knows where he sailed or whether he will return. None has heard since the pure strains of his kantele. But parts of his songs are remembered and sung even now, and most of them you have heard, and the few remaining, if you are eager for them, it may be that one day you shall yet hear.

BOOKS CONSULTED

KALEVALA, *The Land of Heroes*, translated from the Finnish by W. F. Kirby, 2 vols. New York, E. P. Dutton & Co., 1936.

This translation is an almost literal rendering, in un-rhymed metrical verse, of the fifty runes which make up Lönnrot's Kalevala. It was revised by Professor Kaarle Krohn and Madame Aino Malmberg of Helsingfors, who assisted the translator with the excellent notes supplementing the text. The argument to each rune which appears in the original has also been translated, with slight modifications. There is an informative introduction by the translator, and a glossary of Finnish names. The present version is based chiefly upon this work.

THE KALEVALA, *The Epic Poem of Finland*, into English by John Martin Crawford, 2 vols. Cincinnati, The Robert Clarke Co., 1904.

This, the first English translation of Lönnrot's work, was originally published in 1888. It is also a verse rendering. The translator was assisted by several continental and American scholars. His preface embodies the results of his study of Finnish mythology.

Books Consulted

THE TRADITIONAL POETRY OF THE FINNS, by Domenico Comparetti, translated by Isabella M. Anderton, with an introduction by Andrew Lang. New York, Longmans, Green & Co., 1898.

This fascinating work is divided into two parts, one of which deals in scholarly fashion with the traditional poetry of the Finns, epitomizes the contents of the Kalevala, describes Lönnrot's method of composition, and gives a translation, as nearly literal as possible, of one of the main variants of the Sampo runes. The second part of the book is a study of the daemonic and heroic myths of the Ugro-Finnic peoples, and of the runes embodying them. Finally, the author discusses the origins of the other great national epics, contrasting them with the Kalevala.

THE WIZARD OF THE NORTH, by Parker Fillmore. New York, Harcourt, Brace & Co., 1923.

The Finnish epic is here retold briefly in a form suitable for children. The book is provided with a helpful introduction.

THE SAMPO, *A Wonder-Tale of the Old North,* by James Baldwin. New York, Charles Scribner's Sons, 1929.

The author of this book for children, made up of stories taken from the Kalevala, has admittedly altered the original material to suit modern taste, and perhaps for the same reason has employed a style which fails to suggest that of the poem. A few explanatory notes are appended to the volume.

www.ingramcontent.com/pod-product-compliance
Lightning Source LLC
Chambersburg PA
CBHW020833260626
47169CB00003B/958

9798886770056